A Shifter's Tribulations

A Shifter's Tribulations

Shifter's Divinity Series: Book 1
Five Dimension Timeline: Oct, 2017

Fonts: Brushline by Staircase Studio

Cover design by: Saraphinia McCormick
Cover design contains a stock photo, "Dragon Skin"
Copyright © by timbrk

ISBN: 979-8-9999746-0-0

First Edition (October 2025)
1 2 3 4 5 6 7 8 9

Contact info: Saraphinia.dragons@gmail.com

To Purity Culture:
Fuck you

About the Book

This is a reverse harem (RH), dragon shifter, contemporary, romantic fantasy story intended for an adult audience.

This RH is FMMMM, where the female lead has an individual romantic relationship with four men. The four men do not have a romantic relationship with each other.

This book is written in multiple POVs where the FMC's POV is 1st person while everyone else's is 3rd person.

There is mention of teenage pregnancy, pregnancy loss, parental death (Not depicted), family abuse, minor physical torture, PTSD, car crashes, mentions of Christian religion, and sexually explicit scenes between adult characters that include, but are not limited to: Dom/Sub interactions, dragon shifted appendages, raw sex, and sex within hearing distance of others.

This book ends on a cliffhanger!

Reader discretion is advised.

Table of Contents

Chapter One

"LADIES AND GENTLEMEN, WE ARE ABOUT TO start our descent into Memphis. Please make sure to place your tray table up, your seats back in the full, upright position, and have your carry-on baggage securely underneath the seat in front of you or in the overhead compartments. After you're done, make sure to have your seatbelts securely fastened and enjoy the descent. As always, thank you for flying First Edition Airlines, as we know it is your choice to choose comfort over saving money." The male voice came over the speaker. I sat up straighter in my seat, watching out the window. Next to me sat my uncle, Nick, who was being woken up by a stewardess to inform him he needed to put his seat up. It has been two years since I've been home, two years since I've seen my boys. Men, they were now men, and I am now a woman. I'm no longer that helpless 16-year-old girl who struggled to keep up with the Windsor boys. Although I wouldn't have called myself all that helpless at 16, I have grown in more ways than one in the past two years. I caught my hand rubbing my abdomen again. It was a habit I hadn't quite gotten rid of yet, always doing it when feeling anxious.

"We're landing already?" Nick's groggy voice made it evident he wasn't aware of our surroundings yet. While he rubbed the sleep from his eyes, I looked around the plane at the different passengers. They wouldn't be stopping me from being the first one off this plane. It was one of the reasons I chose the first row of seating when buying our tickets.

"It was only a three-hour flight." Three hours too long. I'd done my waiting, and it was time to come home.

"I hate planes." Nick groaned and rubbed his forehead. "Next time, we drive." He sat straighter, popping his neck before tightening his seat belt as if he'd untightened it from when he put it on during takeoff.

"You said that last time." There was no argument about how we would travel from Arizona to Tennessee when travel times were brought up. He could drive all he wanted to, but I ran to buy my plane ticket. There was no stopping me once I was told I was allowed to return. "Besides, there won't be a next time for me." My words left no argument in the matter, but as I looked out the window, I hoped there wouldn't be a next time. If there was a time when my uncle and I had to up and leave again, I'd tell my boys. I would bring the Windsors with me. There was no way I would disappear from their lives again.

"It's not like I had much of a choice either way. You get sick on long car rides." Nick groaned, and as soon as I could see the runway we were about to land on, Nick gripped the armrests, his knuckles turning white, and for a few seconds, I questioned if he was going to tear off the armrests. Why he felt so anxious on airplanes, I never could figure out. It didn't matter how many times he explained it to me. We were dragons for fuck's sake; Flying was what we did for fun. The only reason we weren't flying ourselves across the country was because planes were faster, and there was nothing that was going to make this process of getting back to my boys any longer than it had to be. Three hours on a plane, two for the car ride after, adding a generous hour for time to get baggage and a car rental.

Watching the seatbelt light, the moment it turned off, I jumped over my uncle, grabbed my bag from the overhead compartment, and bolted out of the plane. Nickolas quickly caught up to me, calling my name as we went, trying to get me to slow down. The wait at the baggage claim took longer than it should have. How hard was it to get a bag from the plane onto the conveyor belt? "You'll wear a hole in the ground if you keep pacing like that." Uncle Nick stopped my pacing with a hand on my shoulder. Though I knew, deep down, he meant well, and it was meant to help calm me, it wasn't what I needed. I needed my bright green bag to come down so I could grab it and go. I had to stop myself from jumping on the conveyor when a glimpse of neon green caught my eye. After I grabbed my bag, I felt my stomach drop. Waiting. More waiting as Nick's red bag took another minute to come down, all the while, I couldn't help the grip I had on my bag. If I didn't think I would face consequences for shifting in front of humans and flying home, I would run out the doors right now, but, unfortunately, I was now at the mercy of my uncle's timing. After his bag came down, I knew I had to follow him to the car rental place. I kept on his heels, doing everything I could to get him to hurry without actually telling him to walk faster.

After getting in the car, I was once again left to my thoughts, just as I was on the plane. I started to doubt, doubt if my boys were still mine, whether they wanted to still be mine as I was still theirs. The oldest, Drake, the twins, Henry and Landon, and then the youngest, Asher, who was my age. The four Windsor boys. Those four brothers lived just half a mile across the road from me in Reelfoot Lake State Park, a few minutes away from Tiptonville, Tennessee. All of whom are sons of the only mother figure I had growing up, Mable Windsor. I had to give that woman props, having raised all four of them alone for the majority of it. Their father had passed when Asher and I were only two years old. They lived in a three-story, modern, luxurious mansion with the boy's bedrooms on the second floor and Mable living in the fur-nished basement. I even had my own "guest" room on the third floor because I spent so much time at that house. My home was more of a traditional log cabin with two stories and a storm cellar basement. As much time as I spent over at the Windsor's place, my boys spent just as much at mine growing up. My stomach fluttered, remembering the many nights of throwing all my pillows and blankets down the stairs into the living room and having a movie night, surrounded by the feeling of being protected, as if nothing could hurt me.

Frowning as I realized my hand was once again rubbing my abdomen, I stopped and sat on my hands. I *needed* to rid myself of this stupid habit. One and a half years, it's been since the accident. I shouldn't be so attached still. My heart ached as I thought of the night that started it all..

~*~ ~*~ ~*~ ~*~ ~*~

I walked into my kitchen after having spent the evening with Drake in what we called the cave. A grin plastered on my face; I couldn't rid myself of it if I wanted to. The effect his whispers had on me was something else. Uncle Nick leaned against the kitchen counter with two hastily packed suitcases on the ground next to him. It wasn't until I closed the door behind me that he looked up from his phone. The look he had still haunts me; never before had I seen him so sad, so terrified. "Amelia," I could tell he did his best to keep his composure, though failing at doing so. "We have to take a trip."

Furrowing my brows, I looked at him, trying to see past his words. "A trip?" Taking a couple of steps closer, I stopped as his phone buzzed a few more times in his hands. "A trip where?" My stomach shuddered as I felt like I was going to be sick. I hated seeing my strong uncle look to be on the verge of crying.

"Your grandfather, my dad." I gave him credit for keeping his voice in check. Had we been on the phone, I wouldn't have known something was wrong. "He's invited us over for a trip." Now? I had planned a whole thing for fall break. A week of just me and my boys. "You don't have to go back to school for a bit, so I thought it would be good for you to meet the rest of your family. There's… There's sort of a family reunion happening."

The pounding in my chest went to my head as my thoughts whirled. "And… it can't wait?"

"No, Amelia!" He yelled, hitting his fist on the counter, making me jump. It was completely unlike him to act out like that. "Look, I'm sorry." His hand, not holding the phone, ran through his hair. "But, if we don't leave now, we will miss our flight." He took a breath as he tried to calm down. Nick's eyes filled with unshed tears, gleaming in the kitchen's light.

"I have to tell the boys." It was my first thought as I patted my jean pockets, but realized the phone dropped out of my damned tiny pockets sometime between the Windsor's and my place. Surely there was enough time to run back and get it?

"We are leaving. Now." Uncle Nick grabbed his bag and suitcase before passing me to leave out the front door. I stood there, speechless, surprised at my uncle. Uncle Nick had never really spoken about the rest of our family before. My parents being the single exception, only because I had asked about them so often when I was younger. I stared at the open door and heard the truck door closing before watching him walk back in. "Get in the truck. We are leaving." His words were final as he grabbed my suitcase before following me out the door. It was a silent, tear-filled drive to the airport as I didn't know what to say or ask. Something had pissed off my uncle, and he didn't seem to be willing to talk about it. While we waited for boarding, he took two pills, not heeding the confused look I sent his way.

It wasn't until we were both sitting on the plane that I decided it was okay to ask, "How long is the trip going to be?"

"I don't know." He said apologetically, and I looked away from him; tears once again began to roll down my cheeks as I sent a silent goodbye to my boys, betrayal heavy in my chest.

~*~ ~*~ ~*~ ~*~ ~*~

"We're almost home." My uncle's words broke me out of my thoughts, and I looked around. We'd already gotten off the main road and were now on the dirt road in the forest. I was grateful for it too; my stomach and head were catching up with the present, my head feeling warm to the touch, and my stomach slowly wanting to turn inside out. Out of nerves of seeing them again or due to the long car ride, I didn't know.

Once we got home, there was another half mile I would need to run to get to the Windsor house. As if I were back on the plane waiting for the seatbelt light to turn off and the door to open, I impatiently waited until I felt the magic barrier of my home that I felt was safe enough to jump out of the moving vehicle. Granted, he was about to pull into the drive-way and stop anyway, but there was no waiting anymore. Wasting no more time, I bolted, running on the dirt road that led me to my boys, not caring about the luggage still in the back of the vehicle. I'd help Uncle Nick with it later if he hadn't gotten to it already. My boys needed to know I'm safe. I am home.

Chapter Two

STANDING AT THE FRONT DOOR, MY HEART pounded as my mind whirled. With my fist hovering above the door, everything felt wrong. I should just walk in. Pretend as if these past two years never happened, but I can't. What if they wanted nothing to do with me? What if they hated me? I disappeared without a trace. It was very likely they had moved on. My heart pounded in my ears, all of the sounds of the forest being drowned out by the thump thump… thump thump. My stomach dropped as I felt I no longer belonged here. Was this still home?

A bird came and landed in the bird bath, the splash bringing me out of my head. I looked over to the right and saw the curtains on the kitchen window were closed. So were the ones for the living room to the left of their front door. What if they no longer lived here and someone else took over as park rangers? The thought had never occurred to me until now. With another deep breath, I knocked on the door, hoping it was loud enough for someone inside to hear. If it were Mable or any one of the Windsor boys, they would be able to hear it. Dragon senses tended to be slightly better than the average human's. When the door opened to reveal the wavy red-haired woman, my throat caught. Tears started to sting as I couldn't hold back the relief I felt at seeing the woman who was the biggest mother figure I've ever had.

Mable's expression went from a bright, welcoming smile to utter shock as the stainless-steel bowl full of cookie dough in her arms dropped to the ground with a clang, the tips of her fingers covering her mouth. "Amelia?" She spoke softly, almost unbelievingly. Tears started falling from Mable's eyes, and the woman froze as she looked into my eyes in disbelief.

"I'm home," my voice cracked. Never had I appreciated this woman more than when Mable ignored the cookie dough mess. and wrapped her arms around me in a tight hug. It's what I needed. I squeezed her in turn, never wanting to let go. With everything that has happened these past two years, I didn't want to be anywhere else.

"I can't believe you're here. Come in, come in." Mable urged, pulling me inside before letting go to close the door.

I stopped Mable when she went to bend down to pick up the cookie dough mess. "Here, let me help you with that." I grabbed the bowl and fallen spoon, scooping the chocolate chip cookie dough off the ground. We quickly got the mess cleaned up, and I followed Mable to the kitchen, just off the

10

entryway to the right. The interior had changed slightly, with more pictures on the walls and some knick-knacks that were new or rearranged, but it wasn't cluttered. Mable always knew the secrets on how to keep her house in picture-perfect condition.

"Is Nicholas back too, or is it just you? How long have you been back?" Mable took the bowl from me and put it in the sink. I smelt them before I saw the cookies cooling on a baking sheet on the counter, cooling down along with the ingredients meticulously laid out to make more.

"Yeah, Uncle Nick and I just got in. I ran over while he parked the car." Mable left the bowl in the sink to get another one and started making another batch of cookies, so I took the chance to help and started washing the bowl. Dumping the wasted dough into the expertly hidden trash can in the bottom cupboard to the right of the sink, I smiled. This all felt so natural. "Where are the boys? They're not home, are they?" It was too quiet for them to be here.

Mable giggled. "Do you think I would have cookies cooling down if any of them were home? No, dear, they are in town doing the grocery shopping."

"How are they?" The pounding in my chest came back as I hoped for the best but prepared for the worst.

"Asher graduated back in May and has yet to decide what he is going to do: stay here as one of the rangers or go out and do something else." Mable stopped and looked at me, as if just realizing something. "Oh, honey, I didn't get to see your graduation. Were you in school? Did you have a graduation?"

"No. I did online schooling." I sighed. "I graduated early, actually, and got my diploma in the mail." How much was I ready to tell this woman? I knew I wasn't ready to tell her everything, but she also deserved to know.

"We should do something." Her comment made me laugh. Leave it to Mable to say we should celebrate my graduation rather than celebrate my coming back. I admired her as I didn't need any reminders that I was gone for so long. She knew that. How she knew, I don't know, but I give her all of the props.

"What about Lany and Henry?" I ask, wanting to change the topic.

"Henry started online college so he could stay here to help around the house and still go on patrols. He's studying environmental science. Landon has decided schooling isn't for him and has helped out in different businesses around town, trying out all sorts of jobs to figure out what he wants to do with life." Mable continued to mix the ingredients without saying anything else, starting to concern me.

"And Drake?" Drake was the eldest of the brothers and had the alpha gene. All firstborn dragon shifters are born with the alpha gene, having something to do with our druid magic. As more silence passed, I began to think of the worst. Was he okay? My hands started shaking as I stopped washing the bowl. "Mable?" The woman looked almost sad, lost in her own thoughts. "Is Drake okay?"

"Oh, yes. He's okay, it's just that he…" She trailed off again and shook her head. "The four of them will be back soon, and I think it's best if he tells you." Her answer was concerning, to say the least. What did Drake need to tell me?

Speak of the devil and he shall appear. Loud music came from outside as a vehicle pulled up to the front of the house. I peeked out of the curtain to see a deep green Gladiator, and all four doors opened as soon as it stopped. Asher was the first of them to get out, and I watched as he stopped abruptly, taking in a deep breath. His whole demeanor changed, eyes widening, and he booked it to the front door. I could hear the others complaining to him about something, but Asher ignored their words. I took a sniff of my surroundings as well and could only smell the delectable cookies. They did smell delicious, and it took everything in me not to snag one or two. The only thing stopping me was the fear of a wooden spoon to my hand. The best times to eat chocolate chip cookies are right before and right after they are in the oven.

The front door slammed open, and I could mentally hear Mable's upset words about slamming doors in her house, but the woman kept silent. Asher stopped in the kitchen doorway, freezing when he saw me. "It is you." I blinked, holding back tears at the look in his eyes. Asher was instantly in front of me, picking me up and spinning me around. "You're really here. I'm never letting you go anywhere ever again, Darlin. You're never getting out of my sight." He was just as I remembered him, and my tears of relief fell onto his shirt. A welcoming back with open arms is all I could have ever asked for.

The next one inside was Henry, who came up behind me and sandwiched me between him and Asher, putting his head in the crook of my neck. "Amelia." His voice cracked, and I let out a sob. I could never, would never, leave them again. "Fuck, I've missed you," Henry whispered against my neck.

A thud and rustling made the three of us look over to see groceries in bags having been dropped on the ground. Lany was standing there, frozen. "Holy Fuck." Lany ran over and pushed Asher out of the way so he could hug me too. "Shit, Lia, where have you been?" He quickly moved his hands to my shoulders and looked me over to see if I was injured in any way. After seeing I wasn't currently in any physical danger, he hugged me even tighter.

"Thanks for helping, guys. I know Mable made cookies, but we have perishables." An aggravated, new female voice said as she stepped over the dropped groceries and placed bags on the counter. "Oh, hello." The brunette raised an eyebrow towards me and the boys. "I don't believe we've met yet." She looked me up and down before raising her nose and silently huffing. "I'm Lindsay." Henry growled slightly at the new girl, tightening his grip on me.

"It's nice to meet you. My name is Amelia." I smiled, hearing the front door close.

"Hey, fuck me, right? I know I can carry them all, but are her cookies so important that you couldn't help?" Drake said, his two arms full of the remaining groceries. Looking between Lindsay and me, he walked towards the counter where the other groceries were. Lindsay put her hand on his shoulder.

Her sparkly purple fingernails contrasted with his dark green shirt.

"Yeah. I would say that Amelia is far more important than the groceries." Henry spoke up, stepping out from behind me to stand between Drake and myself. Drake wasn't a threat, was he? Henry sure thought so, and as I glanced at Asher and Lany, they did too. What happened to him while I was away?

"And I would argue that she was already here, and obviously wasn't going anywhere anytime soon, so she could wait, and then, we all could have helped bring in groceries." Lindsay crossed her arms across her chest, making her breasts look slightly bigger. "She could have even helped bring them in." Lindsay tilted her head to the side and raised an eyebrow at me. Who the fuck was this bitch?

The three boys around me growled at Lindsay's words before Drake took a threatening step forward and cleared his throat. I could see the surprise on Drake's face when the others didn't back down from his unspoken threat. This felt wrong. Drake was the last one to see me before I disappeared, so I guess I deserved this. I looked between him and Lindsay, the dots connecting, and I felt my heart split in two. I had to get out of here. I needed air. Clearing my throat, I managed to get words out. "It's nice to see you, too, Drake." He didn't even look at me when I spoke. Knives stabbed my chest at his indifference to me. He'd moved on, I got that, but to outright pretend I was not there was another pain entirely. It was my biggest fear that they would react that way when I returned. "Now," I took a deep breath before looking away from him. "If you don't mind, I still need to go unpack." It felt as if the room was getting smaller and everyone, but Drake, was staring into my soul. I nodded my goodbye, and as I took my first step, Henry spoke up.

"Wait, we'll help you." He grabbed my hand and smiled reassuringly down at me. Asher and Lany quickly came to my side as well. I could feel my throat closing as I wanted to say thank you, but couldn't get it out. I needed to keep it together. I wouldn't break down in front of Drake.

"Mable!" Lindsay said, exasperated, her hands going down to her sides. "Tell your boys to help with putting the groceries away!"

Curious as to how she would act, I looked back at Mable. The older woman cleared her throat, looking at the three youngest of the brothers. "Please, make sure she's taken care of." She smiled and winked at me before Lindsay huffed, crossing her arms once more. "And Drake, if you feel the need to check in on them, you may go also." That made Lindsay's eyes widen, and she grabbed Drake's wrist as if to say he wouldn't be going anywhere.

"I'll be back when I'm unpacked. I can't pass up those cookies." I smiled a sad smile towards Mable and walked out the front door. Tears threatened to fall at the corners of my eyes. Three of the four brothers followed me out and towards my house. Halfway there, I stopped in the middle of the dirt road. "Guys…" I looked at the boys. "I'm sorry. I'm so sorry. I had no choice but to leave. I didn't want to." Asher caught

16

me before I fell to my knees, lifting me and holding me bridal style against his chest before kneeling on the ground. Tears freely fell onto his shirt as I sobbed against him.

"Hey," Henry spoke softly, petting my hair as he crouched down. "You're here now, and we're here for you."

Lany moved my dark hair away from my eyes. "It'll be a little rough transition with the way things have changed, but we're all here for you."

I nodded, thankful for them, and looked up at Asher to see him smiling. "So, you need help unpacking?" His question felt heavier than words. He wasn't just asking about unpacking my clothes. The problem was, there was so much to unpack from the last two years, I didn't know where to start, apart from the night I left, and I couldn't, I wouldn't, without Drake also being there to hear it. Drake was the last one to see me. He probably sought comfort in that Lindsay girl after blaming himself, but I needed to tell him the truth. Unfortunately, I didn't even feel qualified to answer all of their questions. I still had a metric fuck ton of questions.

"Not right now. Maybe if I can have the four of you in the same room without the newcomer, I can talk more."

"Good luck with that." Henry scoffed. "Those two haven't been apart for more than five minutes since they met." As much as I didn't want to hear this, I needed to. "I'm sorry. If it's any consolation, Drake never stopped going on our hunts for you." We started walking towards my house again, Asher still carrying me. "It was shortly after you disappeared." Henry continued. "We were all devastated when we couldn't find any sign of you or your uncle, but it hit Drake the hardest. He kept questioning if you had given him any silent cues of leaving and blamed himself for not noticing. A couple of months into it, we all went into town for a food run before going to search again, and that's when he met her."

Asher's chest rumbled as he spoke. "She's not anything like who I would match him with, and she's nothing like you. Nothing clicked with her for us. That girl just seemed to set her sights on Drake and dug her little claws in, trying to rip him away from us. Fortunately, even though you weren't here, you are the one who kept us together. It was the thought that we couldn't stop looking for you, that someday we'd find you. It's what kept him searching with us, even with her tagging along."

We stood in front of the large wooden cabin, and Asher finally put me down. He kept an arm around me, for which I was utterly grateful. "What are they to each other?" I gathered she was his new lover, but I needed to know exactly what they had going on. I was afraid of the answer, but it was better to hear it now than later from someone else and lose it again.

"They are engaged and have been for about two weeks," Asher spoke angrily. "He didn't even tell us before it happened. They went out for lunch one day, and she came waltzing in, bragging about the ring on her finger. When we asked him about it, he said he felt impulsive, and so they went out and bought a ring. It made Mom so sad when she heard the news that she took our grandmother's ring on our father's side into your room and hid it."

Landon laughed. "Yeah, Mom does not like Lindsay. She's a real bitch, and disrespects Mom as if she's not leagues below Mom."

I nodded, unlocking and opening the front door. "Uncle? We're home!" I went to the kitchen and realized that we needed to go into town for groceries. My back pocket vibrated twice, as if on cue, signaling I got a text.

Uncle: *Went into town for a meeting with my boss at the hospital. I'll bring home some food for dinner, and we can do a grocery run tomorrow if you would like.*

"Looks like we won't have any real food until tomorrow, but Uncle Nick is bringing home food after his meeting." I looked at the three others in the room and pointed across the hall to the living room, where I saw my bag. "My stuff is there."

Henry nodded and grabbed the neon green suitcase while Lany grabbed my backpack. I followed them up the stairs to my room, the other two right on my heels. The room needed a good cleaning; dust had gathered everywhere. "I can't sleep here," I whispered. It wasn't just as I had left it, the drawers open and rifled through. The door to the bathroom open, along with my closet, having evidence someone had searched through it.

"I'm sorry, we tried looking for clues to where you might have gone." Henry sat on my dusty bed, a small cloud puffing up when he did. "We couldn't find anything, though." Asher put his arm around me again, his hand resting on my hip.

"But we have you now, and although we have questions, we know you'll tell us when you're ready." Asher smiled down at me before kissing my forehead.

"I do need to know," Lany spoke up after a moment of silence. "We all need to know… Are you here to stay?" The pain in his voice broke me. It was the exact same pain I've had these past two years.

"Yes." I nodded, looking at the ground. "I didn't want to leave in the first place. I wanted to tell you guys." My voice broke. "I'm sorry." My last words came out as a whisper as it was all I was capable of. With as much heartache and pain as I've gone through, I couldn't imagine what it was like for them, nor could I imagine what kind of Hell or high water I'd go through if I were in their shoes, and one of them went missing without a trace.

Lany nodded. "Then it's on us to help clean this mess up since we created it." He chuckled, trying to make light of the situation.

"I'd appreciate it." I smiled and we all got to organizing the clothes and putting a pile in the corner of the room for laundry. There were several shirts along with almost all of my pants thrown in a donation pile. When I stripped to try on my favorite pair of jeans, I burst into tears when I realized they didn't fit. My hips were too big for them. The worst part is, I couldn't bring myself to explain why I was so emotional about it.

My hips had grown two sizes when I was pregnant. My breasts had also grown a cup. The pain of thinking about that time tore me to shreds, and Henry held me in his arms, rocking me back and forth while Asher and Landon whispered reassuring words, telling me it was okay, that I was even more beautiful in their eyes. It was the pants' fault and not mine. They didn't understand. They couldn't unless I told them, but no words would come out when I tried to speak. I had tried for so long not to cry over my loss, only ever crying while I was alone. I turned to anger so much, choosing revenge over mourning. Anger is so much easier to process than sadness. I know how to process anger. After several minutes of consoling, I was ready enough to finish putting away the clothes that did fit me, and the boys helped bring the laundry downstairs to the washer.

"Do I still have a room at y'all's place?" I was sure I did, but I didn't know the state of that room either. We were all in the living room, and I sat on Asher's lap, my head on his shoulder, and his hand playing with my hair while my legs rested on Henry's lap.

"Of course. Mother changed the sheets and dusted at least once a month, along with your birthday, and your disappearance day. She always wanted to have a place for you when you came back. We all missed you, Lia." Placing a hand on my cheek, he kissed me. It was a soft and quick kiss, but it warmed my heart nonetheless. The boys never used to be so lovey or touchy in front of their siblings before. They all had a mutual agreement to share me, but to stave off any jealous feelings, we kept all public displays of affection to a minimum around the four of them. The fact that the other two didn't bat an eye at any of our touching or kissing showed growth. I just wish it wasn't because I disappeared.

"Thank you." I looked out the window of the living room and smiled. "We need to have a movie night. I just want to be surrounded by you guys tonight and have it be like before." I needed normalcy again.

"That can be done. If you want, since there's no food here, we can have it at our place. You can text Nick, he's invited over for dinner, so he doesn't have to get anything to bring home." We stood up, and I nodded, doing exactly that. It would be good for him and Mable to talk everything out. He'd be much better at explaining things than I would be anyway.

Henry pressed himself behind me, his hands on my hips, and kissed the back of my head. "We can pop some popcorn. We have chocolate and caramel sauce." He whispered into my neck.

Giggling, I looked up to smile at him. "That sounds amazing." We walked out, and I locked the door before looking at the three of them. "Wanna race home?" I barely spoke the last word before Asher started running towards their house. "You cheater!" I called out and saw Henry and Lany shrug at each other before running after their brother. I groan at my disadvantage before running after them.

I surprised myself at how I was able to catch up. Before, when we raced, I was always so far behind them. Black, leathery wings sprouted from my back as I used my wings to help speed up. I passed Henry and was just about to pass Landon when he pulled me to the ground, leaping over me in the process. "Fuck!" I yelled as the rocks scraped up my arms and legs. Two horns protruded from the top of my head, curving towards my face, while shimmering black scales covered my body as I shifted into my dragon form. I was grateful my aunt Carol taught me how to shift while in motion, as I looked back at the three men I passed who had to stop and shift before racing again. My lead didn't last, though, as Henry, a red dragon, and shortly after, Asher, a golden dragon, passed me. I came in third as I landed and then shifted back into my human form. I learned the hard way when my aunt was helping me train my shifting abilities that I shouldn't shift into my human form while going fast. Hitting a tree was much easier in my dragon form than in my human one.

We went to the metal tub disguised as a trash can, and I grabbed out a pair of their sweatpants and tied the string. The boys took out some jeans and put them on. None of us cared enough about shirts to put one on before walking in through the back door of the Windsor mansion.

"I'm sorry, Lia." Landon grabbed my waist and pulled me to him. "Are you okay?" He looked me over. Though I had gotten a few scratches when I shifted, I healed faster, and so there were only red marks on my arms. I noticed his gaze linger on my abdomen and the scar I didn't have before I disappeared.

"I'm okay," I smile, trying to distract him, "But thank you for checking up on me."

"Always." He whispered before kissing me. I wrapped my arms around his shoulders as he licked the bottom of my lip to deepen the kiss.

"Leave room for Jesus." Asher joked, and the kiss broke as we all laughed.

"I'm glad to see you're back." Mable walked into the room. "I just got off the phone with Nick. Is there anything you would like for supper?"

"Everything you make is amazing, Mable. I'll take anything that comes out of that kitchen." I smile and she nods. "I'll see what I can do." The red-haired woman was about to leave, but turned back around to me. "Also, cookies are done. You can have as much as you want. I knew I was making them for a reason. I just didn't know why until you showed up on our doorstep."

"Thank you." I hugged her before we headed to the kitchen. I opened a cabinet for a plate, thankful they were where I remembered them to be. I started plating the cookies on the plate as Henry went to pop the popcorn in the microwave. Asher and Lany sat at the small breakfast table since neither of them were allowed to do any cooking in the kitchen. Mable created that rule after Asher somehow exploded food all over the kitchen and then had to clean it himself, and Lany almost set the house on fire.

"So, what are we watching tonight?" Asher leaned forward.

"I was thinking, maybe a horror movie?" I watched as Lany's eyes shimmered with excitement.

"And where are we going to be watching?" There were several spots we could. There was a home theater, but it had separate seats for everyone, and I didn't want to be separated from them. There was also the living room, but I didn't know how okay Mable would be with moving the furniture. At my house, we'd move the couches in the living room, throw all my pillows and blankets down the stairs, and use the floor. The last option here was my old room. It was the only room with a big enough bed to fit all five of us. Four, I mentally sighed. There would only be four of us tonight.

"Your room." Lany smiled at me, bringing me out of my saddening thoughts.

"My room it is." After I piled half of the three dozen cookies on the plate, the popcorn was popped and put into bowls for us. Asher grabbed the chocolate and caramel sauce, and I followed Henry up the stairs to my room. Unfortunately, when we got to the second story, Lindsay walked out of Drake's room, conveniently, the room closest to the stairs.

"Excuse me." Lindsay's eyes widened as she looked the four of us up and down. "Why the fuck are you topless?!"

Drake walked out of his room, glancing at me before looking at his fiancée. "What's wrong?"

"What's wrong? What's wrong is that she has her breasts out like some whore. I don't need some harlot walking around my house."

"Shut the fuck up." I rolled my eyes. "You better get used to it cunt. I'm not going anywhere, anytime soon. Oh, and if it bothers you so much, leave. Everyone but you in this house has seen me naked before and are all unfazed by it." The chuckles behind me challenged my use of the word. My boys were anything but unfazed by me.

Lindsay scuffed. "Yeah, you're just saying that to make me angry. I'm betting it was when you were all babies, so it didn't matter."

I took a breath and gave the plate of cookies to Landon before taking a step towards Lindsay, causing Drake to give me a warning look. It hurt that he would give me that look, my pulse rising with her adrenaline as I fought off the silent threat. Dating an alpha does have its perks. No one resists their aura when used. "Look, you overgrown excuse of pig skin. I've fucked each and every one of the Windsor brothers, including Drake. Multiple times, in fact, and I don't care if that bothers you. I just told you that if you didn't like me being topless, then you need to leave." I placed my hands on my hips, and Drake put his arm out, stopping Lindsay from getting closer to me. If her looks could kill, I'd be dead. "Now, if you don't mind me, I'm going up to *my* room and having a movie night with *my* boys."

I smirked as I walked away, hearing Lindsay start to complain that I had my own room. It shocked me a bit that Lindsay didn't know about the room. It was the only thing on the third floor. How could she not know about it? Did she think it was just a guest room?

"I wish I could have gotten that on film." Landon laughed as they entered my room. "It would sell millions."

"I don't care if she is Drake's fiancée or not. No one treats me like that, let alone a little nobody." She made my blood boil, and though I tried to brush it off as jealousy, it didn't feel right. Something felt off, almost familiar, and I didn't like it.

"We'll back you up on any fight you want to have with her. She needs it." Asher spoke as he sat on the bed.

"Drake doesn't deserve that. I see the way he looks at her. Hurting her physically will only hurt him too." I hated to admit it, but I could only do verbal spats with her. Maybe I could talk with Drake to help him see the side of her his brothers saw, or to have him tell Lindsay not to be such a bitch. Lindsay was rude to Mable for fuck's sake. The Drake I knew would never let that slide.

The popcorn was placed on the side tables next to where Landon put the cookies, and I went to the bathroom attached to my room. It was just as I remembered it, and taking a look at the jacuzzi tub, I knew I was going to soak and enjoy it when I got the chance. Flashes of times before in that tub made heat shoot to my core. The only one I hadn't had in that tub was Asher. Putting some water on my face, I took a deep breath to cool down. If this was how I felt after a minute around Lindsay, how was I going to coexist with her in the same household?

Going back to my room, I smile as I see Henry scolding Lany for trying to steal cookies before we start watching a movie. "I get the first cookie," I stated as a fact before walking over and grabbing the top cookie. It was still soft and tasted like heaven.

Landon gestured with both hands to me while looking at his brother as if to ask, "Why does she get one?" but we all knew the answer. I smiled, chocolate on the corner of my mouth, and licked it off, looking at the three of them. Asher smiled and shook his head at my antics while Lany pat his lap, and Henry's eyes never left my lips. I crawled onto the bed and laid in between Asher's legs, my back against his abdomen. Asher kissed the top of my head while the other two lay down beside us. Lany put the plate of cookies on my lap, and both Henry and Lany held bowls of popcorn. Henry's had chocolate sauce poured onto the popcorn while Lany's had caramel. I liked both of them, but each boy had his own preference.

Halfway through the movie, I caught myself almost passing out. Lany was caught up in the thrill while Henry looked away at parts. Asher pet my head, playing with my hair, and I fed him cookies when he double-tapped my shoulder every now and then. I couldn't help but want to sleep, though. Asher's chest felt so inviting, warm. I felt safe. I hadn't had a body to fall asleep on for too long, other than my Aunt Carol's occasionally, when she woke me up from nightmares and then held me as I went back to sleep.

"You're not passing out at the best part, are you?" Asher whispered. He could feel my head bobbing as I fought the sleep.

This caused the other two to look back at me, and Henry paused the movie. "We can finish it later, after supper, if you'd like." Henry offered.

"I'm okay." I sat up and rubbed my eyes. The popcorn was mostly gone, and so were the cookies. It was then that the smell of the kitchen wafted into my room, and I could smell the chicken stew Mable was making. It smelled like home.

"Speaking of supper." I could feel Asher's stomach growl. I looked at him, surprised. He'd been snacking on cookies for fuck's sake. Was he still that hungry? Granted, I was hungry enough to eat supper, but Asher's stomach sounded as if it was starving.

"I guess we'd better go see if it's ready." Henry chuckled, and we got out of bed. Thankfully, Lindsay wasn't around when we got down there, but that also meant Drake was nowhere to be found.

"I'm almost done." Mable smiled as the four of us sat down at the table. I checked my phone and saw a text from Uncle Nick.

Uncle: *I was able to get my job again and start tomorrow night. I'll be by to have supper shortly.*

"Will Drake be joining us?" I ask, looking up at Mable.

"Unfortunately, not. I told Lindsay she was not welcome for supper tonight, and they both left. Drake assured me he'd be doing his runs of the lake, so he won't be spending all of his time with her." I held back the disappointment, or, at least, I tried to.

"It will be alright. We'll get him away from her long enough for all of us to talk." Henry hugged me from behind and kissed my cheek. "In the meantime, let's get some real food inside of you."

It wasn't long before Uncle Nick walked through the door, and everyone greeting him before we all sat down to eat. Henry talked about what was new about his classes, and it felt almost normal. I couldn't help but glance at the empty seat from time to time, but with Henry's hand on my thigh, squeezing it reassuringly every time my eyes strayed to the chair, I knew there would be time. Just not now. Yes, I loved all of my boys, but with one missing, it felt off. I knew I hurt that man more than I would know, but I had to have him know it wasn't his fault.

"I don't want to pry too much, but where have you two been? Have you been okay?" The concern wasn't missed from Mable's words.

Thankfully, Uncle Nick spoke up, so I didn't have to. "We were with my father in Arizona." He cleared his throat, clearly uncomfortable.

"Arizona? That's a change." Lany said, looking up at me. He sat across from me, next to Uncle Nick, who sat next to Mable.

"It's much nicer in northern Arizona than in the valley. It's also much less humid than here." I couldn't bring myself to talk about my time in Arizona, not yet. Nick spoke more about the weather than what we actually did there, and for that, I was grateful.

30

"Do people really get this excited about the weather in Arizona?" Asher leaned over to whisper as Uncle Nick continued to talk with Mable.

"Only when it rains." I smile. "Not enough trees for my liking, not even where we were."

"We have all the green you need." Henry put his arm around my shoulder.

"Seriously, though," Asher smiled at me. "We are thrilled to have you back."

"I'm glad to be home. It's where I belong." I smile back and kiss his cheek.

I was done eating before everyone else and excused myself, saying I was going to go to bed. Hugging Mable and my uncle goodnight, the other three said they'd be up soon, and I walked up the stairs. I couldn't help but stop at the second floor and walk down the hall to see what had changed. Drake's room was the first on the left, I knew that already, and I didn't want to intrude on his privacy, so I didn't walk in, despite the temptation to. The room across from his was Asher's. He still had the smiley face carved into his door. I remember the day he did that, just to piss off Drake. It was the day after I lost my virginity to Asher. Admiring it, I also saw today's date, October 2nd. That was new. Or, maybe it was two years old.

Not wanting to go down that trail of thought, I walked further down the hall. The next door on the left was glass and let me see into the darkened office. Henry had changed the room quite a bit, but there was still his father's wooden desk on the left side of the room. Across the hall from Henry's office was the game room. Opening the door, I saw they had the newest gaming console from First Edition Inc. fitted with four virtual reality cubes that someone would stand in and be able to move around on. It was one of First Edition's newest game tech, released only a couple of months ago.

The door opening made me jump, but I relaxed when I saw Asher leaning against the door frame. "Got lost?" he asked.

"I'm making sure I still know my way around the place." Walking to him, I wrap my arms around his waist and rest my head against his chest. "I don't want to feel like a stranger in a home I grew up in," I whispered.

"You're not. Trust me. Now, let's go up to your room and get some sleep. In the morning, we can come up with a game plan to get the gang back together." Asher held my hand as we walked up to my room. Henry and Lany were already in bed, waiting for me.

"There she is." Henry smiled and pulled back the blanket.

Getting into bed and being surrounded by the three of them was what I needed. Landon put a movie on, and I put my head on his chest. It would all be better in the morning.

Chapter Three

Tuesday, October 3rd, 2017

WAKING UP TO THE FEELING OF SOMEONE against my back, an arm around my waist, almost felt foreign. As if I were still in a dream I didn't want to wake up from. He had such a tight hold around me, silently telling me I wasn't going anywhere in his own way. Without opening my eyes, I wiggled closer to the man behind me, to the warmth he radiated. "Good mornin', Darlin'." Asher's sleep-filled voice sent chills down my spine, leaving warmth in between my legs. "Sleep well?" His breath danced across my neck in a way that had me mentally begging for him to kiss me.

"It was the best sleep I've had in years." It was the truth. I was surprised when I realized I hadn't woken up to Henry and Lany leaving the bed. Turning around to face him, I put a leg around his hip. My hands admired his muscles, which involuntarily flexed under my touch. "Where did the other two go?"

"They're out working, playing ranger." Damn, I could listen to this voice all day. His words reminded me, though, that I needed to get back into the rotation.

There was an agreement between the state and our two families. I didn't really understand how it all worked or how it happened in the first place, but we are allowed to live in the state park as long as we protect the wildlife and land in return. Mable ran the visitor center for the most part, taking care of the animals there. The eagles were my favorite, and Mable would often let me help out in their enclosure. The poor animals were rescues, unable to live in the wild. I didn't understand how Uncle Nick kept the agreement while we were away, but it worked out.

Asher got up on his elbow, so he was slightly above me before leaning down and kissing my cheek softly. "Is there anything I can do for you?" His whispered words in my ear brought me back to the present and out of my head.

"I'd love to pretend the last two years never happened." It was something I wished for with all my being. My hand absently went to my abdomen. There was no way I could forget, or pretend it didn't happen, as much as I've tried to block it out of my memory. My throat began to tighten; I could feel my breathing getting shallow. It didn't matter that I knew I wasn't back there, that I was safe. My body believed otherwise.

"I can do that." Asher's gruff voice danced across my neck, thankfully bringing me back to the present. "But I need to hear it from your lips." His hand trailed from the underside of my breast down to my waist, causing me to move my hand so he could continue.

"Asher," the name was more like a breath than anything.

"Amelia." He whispered before kissing my neck softly. The feeling of his teeth shifting to fangs had me forgetting how to breathe for a second.

"I need you," I spoke, reminiscent of our first time together. "I want you. Please. I need you inside me." He leaned back enough to lock eyes with me. "If you'll have me."

"I will always have you." I hardly let him finish before leaning up and kissing him. His hand trailed down, in between my legs. The groan he let out when he felt how wet I was for him was intoxicating, sending more warmth down my spine. "Oh, fuck." With a slow insert of a single finger, I whimpered. His growing erection pressed against my leg. He pulled his finger out before bringing it to his lips and sucking. "You taste better than I remember."

His eyes briefly flashed red, his pupils turning to slits. It was the hunger of his dragon, the look I craved from each of the Windsor men. A whimper escaped my lips when his hand went back under my sweatpants, and as his fingers began to rub at my entrance. His mouth came down to one of my breasts, sucking and lightly biting on the nipple. "Asher." I moaned. "Please, I want-." My words hitched as his two fingers slipped into me and moved with a come-hither motion.

"I need you." With my words, he growled against my breast. Trailing kisses from one to the other, he gave my other breast the same attention, adding his thumb to rub that bundle of nerves. "Asher!" I bucked my hips, but his other hand kept me in place against the bed.

"Yes, my darlin'?" He looked up at me.

"More." I got out with another moan. "I need more."

"Whatever you wish." Asher moved between my legs, removing his fingers from me before ripping my sweatpants with his claws and throwing them across the room. "Is this what you want?" He smirked as he started to kiss up my thigh, giving me small bites occasionally. Sparks of pleasure ran up my legs from his kisses, and I could feel as I got even wetter. "May I eat your delicious pussy?" He growled, his lips inches away from where I wanted them. Asher took his time as he inhaled my scent.

"Anytime you want." My hands went to the back of his head to grab his wavy, red tresses. Anything to encourage him to continue.

"You're beautiful, Darlin'." He licked my entrance, his claws slightly digging into my hips to hold me still. His eyes were now permanently slitted red orbs, heated with desire. Asher flicked his tongue out. It shifted too, teasing me with the forked end, not touching my clit but licking around it.

I didn't bother hiding my moans; the only one I'd be concerned about hearing them was, at worst, two floors down. "Fuck me. Please."

"But I need to eat breakfast first." Asher began sucking my clit and put two fingers inside me, causing my back to arch. Pressure built inside of me as I moved my hips, grinding against his mouth. My moans got louder with every movement of his fingers, bringing me closer to cumming. The pleasure built until the damn burst, and I came, squirting on his face. He growled against me, licking all of my juices off me before licking his lips and smiling at me. "So good. So…" His voice trailed off as he looked me up and down. "Beautiful."

I could tell he saw the horizontal scar from the accident from almost two years ago. If he was curious, he didn't ask about it, and for that, I was grateful. I wasn't ready to hash that out.

I watched as he got up and undid his jeans, his hard cock flopping out. I bit my lip, wanting it, needing it desperately. "Yes, please."

Downstairs, Lindsay groaned, annoyed she was woken up. Feeling around for the man beside her, she opened her eyes, realizing he wasn't there. She paused for a moment, settling the slight panic at the back of her mind. It was then that she heard the sound of the shower coming from the bathroom. With a smirk, she stripped, tiptoeing to the bathroom door. Just before she touched the handle, the brown-haired woman heard the moans and cries of the youngest Windsor's name from above her coming out of the vent. Lindsay could even make out the words the bitch was moaning. "That whore. I've worked so hard for him, and she thinks she can just waltz back in his life? She probably thinks sleeping with his brothers will make him jealous." Lindsay scoffed.

Opening the door, she walked in proudly, but once again stopped when she noticed the harlot's moans were even clearer in the bathroom, echoing off the walls. Quickly pulling back the shower curtain, she saw Drake leaning against the marble wall, water splashing his muscled chest, and his head tilted back as his hand jerked his cock. The alpha's groans of pleasure mixed with growls. Every now and then, red and golden scales started to appear on his chest and arms before rapidly disappearing.

The sudden temperature change brought Drake back to his surroundings as he opened his eyes and saw his fiancée. His eyes changed from slits to more round, human pupils instantly. Her face quickly turned red in anger.

"Babe, wait." He followed the stomping woman out of the bathroom, water dripping down his form, dick still hard, though getting softer due to the chill of his bedroom. Lindsay stopped, took a deep breath, and turned around to face the man. "I can explain."

Her anger was suddenly, completely gone from her face as she smiled mischievously before switching to innocence. "It's okay, daddy. You don't have to explain." Lindsay grabbed his hand, smiling. Her hand traveled up his arm to his shoulder, and she could feel him relax under her touch.

"You can jerk off anytime you feel the need for relief." Standing on her tiptoes and both hands on his shoulders, she got close to his ear. "Just make sure you cum to me and not the whore your brothers have decided to have."

"I would never. I will always protect you." Drake smiled softly and pecked the cheek of the woman in front of him. "Now, if you don't mind, I'm going to get ready for work."

Amelia

"Are you ready?" Asher aligned his cock with my entrance, and I took a second to admire his chest before nodding. "I need you to say it."

"Yes. I want you to fuck me." I hardly finished my sentence when he slammed his rock-hard cock inside me, filling me. "Fuck, Yes!" My hips moving on their own accord. This is exactly what I needed, what I've been missing these past two years.

"Fuck, you're so good." He pulled out slowly and then slammed back into me, hitting that spot deep inside me I could never get on my own. I wrapped my legs around him, not wanting him to pull out so much, but that didn't stop him. The tip of his cock was still inside of me the next time he pulled out before thrusting hard.

"More," I asked, "please."

Asher bent down, his lips touching my ear. "Never leave me." It sounded like a plea more than a demand. "Promise you'll stay."

It was that moment I felt how much he'd been hurt by my disappearance. "I promise." I pulled his head back to lock eyes with him. "I won't leave you. I love you." I lean up and kiss him, doing my best to convey how much I missed him, too. His thrust got faster, but he didn't let up on how hard he was thrusting. Horns slowly grew from his temples, naturally slicking backwards. I could feel another orgasm growing inside of me. "Asher. Fuck, I'm close." My hands grabbed his horns, loving the sounds coming from him.

"Cum for me, Darlin." He growled. "Cum on my cock." I did as he said, crying out his name while my muscles spasmed around his cock. He didn't let up, instead going faster, letting me ride out my orgasm while building to his own climax. "In or out?" He asked.

Flashes of blood came across my eyes at the question. Sounds of broken glass and yelling flooded my senses, clearing my lust-filled brain. It was sobering, and he stopped moving, obviously concerned about my sudden change of demeanor.

"Amelia?" He asked, concern flooding his voice.

I had to hold back tears as I shook my head. Closing my eyes. "Out." I managed to get out, and he pulled out, just in time to cum on my stomach.

Breathe. In… Out… In… Out… Deep, calming breaths. The sound of running water helped. "Here." A male voice spoke before I felt a cool rag, cleaning me up. I opened my eyes to see Asher, concerned and making sure I was all clean. After he tossed the rag into the laundry, he crawled into bed next to me and held me. He didn't ask what was wrong or why I suddenly had such a change; he probably assumed I had been raped while I was away to cause this reaction. Nope. The implications of cumming inside of me, when I knew I wasn't on birth control, were dangerous. I've done that tango before. I didn't want to go through that again.

"Did you want a shower?" He kissed the back of my neck. "I'll clean you if you'd like, or if you want to be alone, I'd be okay with that too. Just tell me what you need."

"I'm good." It was a lie; we both knew that. I was not good, but I will be okay. The mantra I lived by for the past two years. Things pass, it's up to me to decide how I react to it. "I'm kinda hungry. You shower, don't let me stop you." I sat up, and he leaned down, kissing my forehead.

"If you're sure." I nod and smile up at him. It was a half-smile, not all of it reaching my eyes. How he treated me made me want to cry. I don't deserve the love he was giving me. I couldn't even keep what remnant I had of my boys alive. "I love you," Asher whispered against my forehead. "I'll be down in a few minutes." Asher disappeared behind the bathroom door.

Deep, calming breaths. I needed to keep breathing. I can get through this. With those thoughts, I got dressed in a simple white sundress with flowers scattered on it, as it was all that fit me in this closet anymore, stopping just under my ass.

Walking downstairs, I hesitated at the second floor, taking moments to look at Drake's door. I couldn't stand the hole in my chest at his absence, but was he ready? As much as it tore my chest apart, I knew our talk would only happen in his time. If Drake didn't want to acknowledge my existence, I wouldn't push for it. He needed to heal just as much, if not more than I still do. Taking a deep breath, I continued down the stairs and into the kitchen.

It was the silence of the house that helped me calm my mind. I used to hate the silence, but as I sat there, at the breakfast table in the corner of the kitchen, eating my fruity cereal, the silence allowed my thoughts to sort themselves out. I might not be okay right now, but I will be. The dust is still in the air and needs to settle.

At the sound of footsteps, I knew who was walking down the stairs. My boys don't have such light footsteps, and Mable doesn't go upstairs. Upstairs was the boys' space, and Mable raised them right, having them take care of their own space. The ground floor was a shared space, while the basement was Mable's. It was shortly after puberty when I stopped going down there. Our girl time was spent more at the visitor center than in her space when I started middle school.

Mentally wishing for Lindsay to walk out the front door or do as Drake did and ignore me completely, I suddenly found a spot on the table that was the most interesting thing in the world to look at. "Hey." Lindsay smiled and pulled out the chair on the other side of the small, round breakfast table. "I think we got off on the wrong foot." I looked up at her, wanting her to disappear. The energy radiating off her made me want to vomit, making me lose my appetite. "Drake explained everything to me. I'm sorry." She put her hands on the table, leaning forward. "First impressions are almost always wrong. Let me redo this." She put one of her hands up for me to shake. "My name is Lindsay."

Looking at her hand, the shiny diamonds covering the band on her ring finger glistened. "I have also been told about you." I inwardly smiled at how bland my voice sounded. No malice, no jealousy, no happiness. I took another bite of my cereal, despite my stomach doing flips. Looking the woman across from me up and down, I shrug. "Just don't be a bitch. Don't be a bitch to me, to my boys, and don't *ever* think about being a bitch to Mable." The look in Lindsay's eyes went from shock to seething as I mentioned Mable. "Don't be a bitch, and we can get along swimmingly." I did my best to hold back the sarcasm.

The seething look Lindsay gave me flipped, like a light switch, to the friendliest mask. "Deal." She gave her offered hand a little shake as a gesture for me to try and shake her hand.

I ignored her hand, knowing it would annoy her. A handshake was such an innocent, welcoming gesture, but the idea of touching her at all sent chills down my back. "What do you do for work? I leaned back, bringing my bowl closer to me.

Lindsay blinked a few times before pressing her lips together, failing to hide her irritation at not having her hand shaken. "I work for my parents. There's a small bakery in town that we run."

"Just the three of you?" I raise an eyebrow, hiding my amusement at the other female's confusion.

"Yes. Why?"

"I'm just curious." Drinking the milk from the bowl before setting it down, I looked around before looking at Lindsay again. "How much money do you make at the small shop?"

I could see the moment her friendly mask broke. "How dare you accuse me of gold-digging!" Slamming her hands on the table, Lindsay stood up. "I don't care about his money."

"How much was the ring?" I nodded to her hand.

Lindsay tipped the chair over and stormed out the front door, slamming it behind her. I would need to apologize to Mable later for the door slamming. I went to the sink, rinsing my bowl. Another set of footsteps made me freeze. I didn't need to look behind me to see that it was Drake coming down. "I'm sure Henry and Landon will be done with their patrol soon." Hearing his voice made my heart beat faster. Suddenly, Drake was at my back, his chest against me and his hands on mine, taking my bowl from my hands. His sleeves were rolled up to just below his elbows. "We should head out before they return." He backed up and put my bowl and spoon in the dishwasher. I turned around, my words having been taken from me. Why speak to me now? Why press against me like that when he had a fiancée?

"Are... Are you talking to me?" Taking a step back, I needed to calm my breathing. He acted so casually.

Drake looked at me before looking around, as if there was anyone else in the room he could have been talking to.

"Yes." His hand went up and down, gesturing towards me. "Why are you dressed like that? The others are about to be home."

"Why does it matter to you what I wear?" My eyebrows scrunched together. What was happening?

"I thought-." His sentence cut off when the front door opened. Drake took a protective stance in front of me when Henry and Landon walked in, only wearing boxers. The two stopped abruptly when they saw us.

"Are we intruding?" Henry asked, looking at me with an arm out to stop Lany from taking a step forward. I looked at them both, Lany close to snarling at his oldest brother.

"Yes." Drake crossed his arms.

"No," I say at the same time.

"You don't have to be nice to them. Let's go." Drake walked away from his brothers, using the door on the other side of the kitchen. The oldest Windsor male stopped when he realized I hadn't followed him.

"Go with him." Henry encouraged in understanding. I nodded, not entirely sure of what was happening but realizing this might be the only time I would get alone with Drake.

I followed him until we hit the tree line. "Drake, wait." The blonde stopped, turning to look at me. So many questions ran through my mind, but before I could get any questions out, I needed to apologize. He needed to know. "Drake, I'm sorry." My eyes started to burn as they began to water. I took a deep breath, knowing I had to get this out, and there was no way I would be able to speak if I was crying. "I'm sorry I left like that. I'm sorry I didn't say goodbye. I didn't have a choice. It wasn't your fault." My voice cracked, betraying me. Tears started to fall, and I didn't wipe them away. He needed to see. "I'm sorry I couldn't…" Drake took quick strides towards me, holding me tightly as I cried. His strong arms making me feel safe.

"Shh," He whispered, using his alpha presence to help calm me. It helped, but didn't make the tears stop. "Baby." He spoke against my hair. "It's alright. It's my fault." His words only made me cry harder. It wasn't his fault. He did nothing wrong. "I don't blame you. I'm not angry at you." He kissed my forehead and pet my hair lightly. "It's alright." Drake picked me up, walking to the lake, not too far from here.

At the mention of his anger, I recalled how he treated his brothers. Why was he upset at them? "What was that about, inside?"

"What was what about?" His confusion was evident in his eyes.

"In the kitchen, your brothers… are you fighting with them? You've never treated them so coldly."

Drake's calm and comforting demeanor quickly changed to one of anger. "They don't deserve to be treated nicely, not after what they did; not after how they made you feel."

How they made me feel? What the hell was he talking about? "What do you mean?" I took a glance behind Drake towards the house that was slowly getting covered with more and more trees as we walked further away. Did he suddenly blame his brothers for my disappearance?

Drake blew smoke from his nose, the smell of a campfire surrounding us, and a low growl rumbled through his chest. I looked up at him to see his golden eyes glowing with flames flickering across them, pupils slitted. "They betrayed you."

Chapter Four

ASHER

ASHER, A TOWEL AROUND HIS WAIST, WALKED down towards his room when he overheard his brothers talking in Henry's office. "I really hope she gets answers from him. I'm surprised he acted that way while she was around." Henry sat behind his large wooden desk with Landon on the other side.

"What happened?" Asher stepped into the room, closing the door behind him.

The two others looked up, and Henry took a deep breath in, catching the scent of Amelia all over his brother. "Fitting." He smirked at his youngest brother, who rolled his eyes.

"Like you two didn't know what was going to happen when you left this morning." Asher smiled and walked over to the bay window across from the door. Looking out the window, he looked from the tree line outwards towards the vast forest.

Landon leaned back in his seat. "It would be you who had her first again." With his hands behind his head, he regaled Asher of the concerning occurrence in the kitchen.

It took a few moments for Asher to think about it. "And Lindsay wasn't around at all?"

"No. We don't know where she ran off to, but she wasn't around when it happened."

"Maybe he wanted to speak with her alone. If Lindsay wasn't there to stop them from having a talk, maybe it was the only way he could think of to get alone time with her without anyone intruding. A lot is going through his mind, and you both know how much he's had to heal. What if he just needs closure, and talking with her is how he can get it? If anything, she could probably get some answers from him."

Amelia

Drake stopped when he got to the lake and set me down. I took a step back from the fuming alpha. "What do you mean they betrayed me?" Reasons flooded my mind. Still not knowing why Uncle Nick and I had to leave so suddenly, the worst came to mind. Were the others the reason I had to disappear so suddenly? Was that why I wasn't allowed to say goodbye?

If Drake knew that, why would he stay so silent when I came back, allowing his brothers to be so close to me? Maybe his brothers did something without them knowing they did. I could feel my heart pounding and echoes of doubts coming to mind. Looking back at Drake, my tearful eyes locked with the fire in his.

Drake shook his head. "They disowned you." He hugged me again. The words felt wrong as I heard them, but with how drastically Drake was reacting, he was telling the truth. "Rejected you." He kissed my head again. "But I'm here to keep you safe and make sure they don't harm you."

Nothing made sense anymore. If Drake was telling the truth, were the others lying to me? "Why have they been so nice to me then?" Were they planning something against me? It didn't sound like them. This didn't sound like Drake either. How much has changed since I disappeared?

"I don't know." He leaned back, moving one of his fingers under my chin to make me look up at him. "They might be planning something against you. You must stay with me, though. Don't leave my side, especially while they are around." If my heartbeat were any faster, it would burst out of my chest. Being so close brought back so many memories, and it broke my heart even more knowing he belonged to someone else now.

Exhausted. I felt exhausted. Too many emotions whirling through my head, too many thoughts thinking about what might have been, what might be. I have shed too many tears since coming back. I turned away from him and looked at the lake. We started walking around the lake on the trail in silence, allowing me to process what had all been said. It had to be true. There would be no reason for Drake to lie to me, would there? Would he lie to me because he hated me so much and wanted to ruin me? That was also something the Drake I knew wouldn't do. No, if there was a problem, Drake was the first one to corner me in a room and hash it out. He always allowed me time to process, but he was also always in the room when I did.

It all hit me at once. I broke down, stopping and going to my knees, sobbing. I knew nothing. I didn't know what caused Uncle Nick and me to suddenly have to go to Arizona without telling anyone. I didn't know what my boys did. I didn't know if they were still mine or not, if they had done something to hurt me or not. "I know, Baby." Drake soothed me, sitting on the ground and holding me in his lap. "They hurt you." He whispered. "But we don't have to go back. We can go to your place, grab a sweet treat." I looked out at the lake, just a few feet away. "We can have your mom make your favorite." The water's movement soothed me, calmed me more than his words did. If I was being completely honest, I wasn't really listening to his words, more of the cadence he spoke in. Focusing on the water's movement, I remembered the summers with my boys on a boat. The last time I was at the lake, I was with the man who was holding me now. Hours before I disappeared from their life. Drake and I went off the beaten path, passing through the kudzu's blanket and into our own wonderland.

Drake wiped away my drying tears as I calmed down. "Thank you." I smiled up at him.

"What's wrong?" He looked down at my hand.

I was caught rubbing my abdomen. Shit, I needed to figure out another way to self-soothe. "Oh, it's noth-." Drake spoke before I could finish.

"Where's your ring?" He looked at my hand and then at me before looking up at the sound of someone approaching.

Lindsay walked towards us, a smile on her face, and then her eyes widened as she looked at her hand and blushed. "Oh, I got it dirty at the bakery, so I dropped it off to get cleaned." How in the hell did she find us? Yes, we were sitting just off the path, but fuck, we could have been anywhere, and yet, here the bitch was. "What are you two doing out here? Alone?" Lindsay took an exasperated sigh. "And your dress hardly covering your ass."

I didn't need this. I stood, putting my hands on my hips. "I haven't changed since you and I talked in the kitchen."

"You should wear less revealing clothing," Drake said, standing and taking a step away from me. "Don't want my babe to get the wrong idea about you and me." He then walked up to Lindsay and kissed her. She, in return, put a hand against his cheek, beckoning him further into the kiss.

Yeah, I didn't need this. Hopelessness filled me, and I couldn't watch this. "I'll be going then." I half expected Drake to tell me to stay, that he needed to make sure his brothers didn't hurt me. One look from Lindsay, and I knew Drake wouldn't say a thing. She had him too tightly around her finger. It truly felt as if I had been stabbed in the heart four times today, losing each and every one of my boys. Once I was out of eyesight, I ran, shifting into my dragon and flying home. Could I even call it that anymore? Nothing felt like home. Arizona didn't feel like home; it was more like a prison for two years. Here was no longer home, my boys gone. Once I got to my cabin, I shifted back to my human form, putting on some boxer shorts from the clothes bin outside and heading through the back door.

"Uncle Nick?" I called out, doing my best to compose myself.

"In my room!" When I walked in, I saw him putting his dress shirts on hangers before hanging them up, but if he wore those shirts every day, could they be considered dress shirts? "What's up?"

"When did you want to go into town for groceries?" Other questions echoed in my mind. What caused us to leave so abruptly? Why were we allowed back now? What did the Windsors have to do with it? I wanted to give him the third degree, but I knew, after years of trying, I wouldn't get the answers with direct questions.

"Oh, I don't know. We could go when I'm done hanging up the last of my shirts if you want." He hung up another long-sleeved button-down.

"I'd like that." I walked upstairs to my room to change into a pair of jean shorts I brought and a black tank top, not bothering with a bra. Who cared if the outline of my nipples would be showing? Their opinion didn't matter. Slipping on a pair of flip-flops, I returned downstairs and waited on the couch in the living room, my mind wandering to what the other three might be doing right now. Would they care if Drake returned to the house, and I wasn't with him? What would they think? What would they do? Did I want to hear them out? Interrogate them about what Drake said? If I were honest with myself, I wasn't ready for that.

"You ready?" Nick checked his pockets for his phone, in his back left pocket, wallet, in his back right pocket, and keys, in his front left.

"As I'll ever be." I put on a fake smile and walked out to the vehicle, getting in the passenger's side.

"I still don't completely understand why you don't want your own vehicle," Nick said, starting the car and heading down the dirt road. "You wouldn't need to keep buying new clothes if you drove instead of flying." It was true, it was also not the first time we've had this talk. I hated cars. I hated them before the accident, and I despise them even more now. My heart raced anytime it felt like we were going too fast. If Uncle Nick didn't break as soon as I thought he should, I would feel my throat start closing, and I could hardly breathe. I didn't need my own vehicle. I didn't want to be in a moving vehicle, let alone drive one.

If my aunt, Carol, were here, she would back me up and talk about how it was better for the environment to fly rather than drive. Uncle Nick would then retort, saying something about how cars aren't what they used to be. As I understand it, most cars nowadays are either powered by a steam engine, running on saltwater, or solar and wind-powered. The transition to renewable energy was started by First Edition Inc. a few years back. They proved a major company could still profit while running solely on renewable resources, and all the other big corporations followed in their wake, causing a second industrial revolution.

"Uncle Nick?" I started as we approached the farmer's market. I knew now wasn't the best time to ask, but with how the day was going, why not? "Why haven't you told me what caused us to leave here?"

He sighed and rubbed his head, stalling his answer. "I knew you'd go looking for it. Especially after seeing what you did when you lost-"

"Don't," I cut him off, glaring at him. I didn't need a reminder, let alone hear it out loud.

He put his hand up in surrender. "After I saw what you did to find those men who attacked you, I knew if I told you why we left, you would go off and get yourself killed."

"Would you be able to tell me now?" I leaned forward. "Whatever this ominous threat is, it's gone. Isn't it?" Uncle Nick was right about one thing. Whatever the threat was, my boys or something else, it would pay. I would make it my mission to hunt it down and make it pay for ruining my life. It wasn't like I had anything to lose now. Uncle Nick could move back to Arizona with the family. The Windsors had obviously gotten along without me. No, whatever or whoever had caused my life to be ruined would suffer at my hands.

"Amelia." He sighed. "The threat is gone. There's no need to know."

"If the threat is gone, there shouldn't be any reason for me not to know." I slumped in the seat, staring out the window.

"How was your night over at the Windsors?"

"Fine, just peachy." I didn't care how sarcastic it sounded. The memory of my night, of my morning after, was ruined because of my walk with Drake. "Drake is engaged."

"Mable said something along those lines. Good for him…" His voice trailed off, and I could feel his eyes on me. "I'm sorry, Honey. How are the other boys?"

"I said they're FINE." The temptation to jump out of the moving vehicle was getting harder to resist. I wouldn't get too hurt if I shifted while I jumped. I could use my wings to wrap around me and have my scales protect me. I would also heal faster if I did that.

"Okay, I won't ask." The car ride was silent after his words, and I wasn't going to be the one to break the silence.

We pulled up and parked; the farmer's market was busier than I remember it being from before. There were a few faces I recognized, and they waved; I smiled and nodded. I wasn't in the mood to talk to anyone. Nick went to talk to the butcher, and it was up to me to buy the fruits and vegetables. "Watch where you're going!" I glared at the tall, bleach-blonde, middle-aged man who bumped into me, causing me to drop a bag of vegetables. He, too, dropped a few of his things.

"I'm sorry, ma'am. I didn't see you there." He apologized, chuckling awkwardly. Here, let me help you." The man grabbed a couple of ears of corn and handed them to me to put in my bag. After everything was picked up, we stood, and I brushed the dirt off my knees. "Forgive me, but I don't believe I've seen you around here before."

Looking him up and down, he didn't seem armed, his mannerisms weren't hostile, but there was something about him that was off. I could probably take him on in hand-to-hand combat, though, so I disregarded the feeling. "I just moved back here."

"Then let me introduce myself. My name is Alvin, Alvin Hermig." He did a slight bow of his head.

"Amelia." I put my bag over my shoulder, looking at the stand to my right, hoping that if I acted normal, he'd walk away and leave me alone.

"That's a pretty name. It's nice to meet you." He put his arm around my shoulders, putting his hand on my right shoulder, and leaned into my personal space, as he pointed at the basket of pears. "Those are the fresh ones."

I wanted to puke. My head began to hurt, a numbness started at the back of my head. I felt gross. I dramatically shrugged him off me, yelling at him. "Don't fucking touch me!" The people around us started to look at us, causing Alvin to take a step back and look at me as if he were the victim.

"I'm sorry. I meant no harm. I just thought you would want to know that those are the good pears. Just trying to help."

The elderly man behind the stand smiled at me. "He would know; he buys a bundle of them every week for his signature pear cobbler." Shaking my head at the dismissal of the situation, I walked away. I didn't want to be around people if they saw nothing wrong with what just happened. As I walked, my headache went away, but I still felt like I needed a shower. I had enough fruits and vegetables to last the week, so I went to wait in the car. Thankfully, it wasn't too much of a wait until Uncle Nick came back with freshly cut meats and a couple loaves of bread.

It was a quiet ride home. He didn't ask how I was or try small talk. I wasn't in the mood to talk either, working through my thoughts and emotions. When we pulled up, I finally found my voice. "I want a job."

"We do need to set you up on a patrol, don't we?" Uncle Nick looked up, pondering. "We can do that after we put away the food." Loading our arms with what we could carry, we started walking inside.

I didn't want that job. Being around the boys would hurt too much. "Does it have to be that job? How is it possible you work at the hospital instead of doing patrols? I know Mable works at the visitor center in order to not do them, but the hospital has nothing to do with the park. How did we even keep this house when we haven't been here for two damn years?" My volume grew with each sentence until I was yelling. "You tell me nothing about anything serious. I should know by now what was so bad here that it had to ruin my life!" Involuntary tears fell from my eyes. I wasn't sad. I was pissed. "I lose my boys and then my child, and now, two years later, I find out that three of my boys had something to do with causing me to leave! Is that why you won't tell me? Because it was the Windsors? Why the fuck would we come back then? Why the fuck would you allow me to be alone with them?" Nothing made sense anymore.

He walked closer to hold me. "Amelia, hold on a second." He held me tightly as I sobbed into his shoulder, wanting nothing more than to punch something, but knowing I didn't want to hurt him. "What are you talking about? The Windsors had nothing to do with it. Where did you get that idea?"

"Drake told me," I spoke against his chest.

"Why would he think that?" Nick brought me to the living room and sat down on the couch, having me sit next to him.

"He said his brothers betrayed and disowned me. What else would that involve?"

"Maybe they were hurt after you left and were mad, saying things they didn't mean. You really should talk to the four of them at the same time."

"I can't. I was lucky enough to get 10 minutes with Drake without his fiancée there. It's like I turn invisible when she's around him." I didn't like to say it often, but my uncle was right. Replaying my conversation in my mind, Drake never did say how his brothers betrayed me. I just didn't see a way for me to talk to him again.

"Try to find out the times she is typically away from Drake and bring him in a meeting with his brothers so you all can come to an understanding." Nick rubbed my back as I started to calm down. Deep breaths. In... Out... "If you would like, I can come with you, and I could call Mable asking if we could all have dinner together again, have a deeper discussion this time.

Nodding, I took another deep breath. Nick smiled and held me until I was the first to pull away. He then called Mable, setting up our dinner tonight.

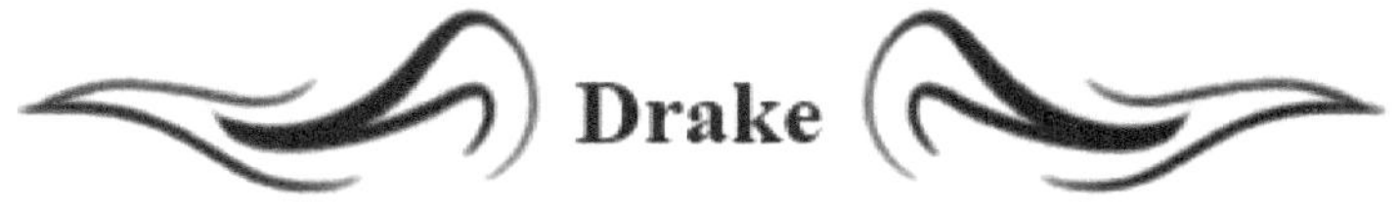

Drake

A few hours later, Henry, Landon, and Asher were in the VR room, headsets and sensors on their limbs. The three of them walked on their circular treadmill as they made their way through the VR post-apocalyptic city. The 3rd person views of the game shown on the wall in front of them via a projector from the ceiling. Henry crouched down as he heard footsteps. "Hold." He whispered. The other two stopped just behind their brother behind a building. He pulled the handgun out from his side and looked back, his brothers mimicking his movements. "On 3. One..." He put a finger up. "Two..." Before he could say 3, the game showed, in bold red lettering, the word "paused". That only meant one thing: someone had opened the door to the room. The pause feature was optional, but they thought it wise to be more aware of their surroundings if someone they didn't want to come in did so. They all took off their headsets to see Drake at the door.

"Mother says we have guests coming over and she needs your help in getting the dining room set up." Drake waited for them to take off their VR sensors before having them follow him downstairs to the dining room. Similar to last night, the table had been elongated to fit 8 comfortably, just to fit all of the food Mable prepared.

The meat had already been placed, and they saw Mable next to the table as they walked through the double pivot doors. "Oh, good, Asher, could you set the table for seven? Henry, get out the drinks and extra napkins. Landon, I need you to help me bring more food out." She didn't pause while she spoke, expertly placing the plates of food down. They all followed their orders, Drake standing there confused.

"Mother, why seven?" He recounted the chairs at the table again to make sure he wasn't miscounting.

"The five of us and our two guests."

"Shouldn't my future mate be here as well?" He put his hands on his hips and puffed his chest out slightly, the stance showing how serious he was since he wouldn't dare use his alpha presence on his mother.

"No." She stood her ground. Mable knew Lindsay shouldn't be here for this dinner, and if she had any say in it, the girl wouldn't be attending any of the future dinners. Even from the short interaction she witnessed with Amelia and Drake while Lindsay was around, Mable could tell something was wrong with her son.

"And why not?" Drake knew the anger in him was seeping into his words, unable to control it. Maybe he needed to shift and fly for a few hours; a good fuck could calm him down too. The thought of his woman riding him made him smirk, but then he blinked and looked at his mother, coming back to the present. She had a brow raised with one arm on her hip, the other resting on the table. "Apologies, Mother. May I be excused from the dinner in that case?" It didn't matter that he was alpha; he knew the woman in front of him could rain Hell if she wanted to. Drake knew when his mother was in charge and accepted that in the family dynamic.

"No, you may not. This is a very important dinner you and your brothers need to attend. You can call your girl and explain, you are needed for important business and therefore she is not welcome over tonight." She left no more room for argument, and his brothers entered the room with the items they were told to gather.

"I hope these guests are worth it." Drake stalked out of the room to his bedroom, changing into a dressier set of clothes. He put on a black, button-up, long-sleeve top and rolled up the sleeves to just below his elbows. Drake then put on his jeans and tucked in his shirt before putting his belt on. Looking in the mirror, he splashed some water on his face, his head starting to hurt. It made him groan, grabbing his temples. "Fucking Hell." He cursed under his breath. The thudding in his head matched the heartbeat in his chest.

Pulling out his phone, he scrolled to the contact "Mate" and pressed call. It was strange when she didn't pick up. She always picked up. He left a voicemail, hoping she was alright, and mentally took note to call back in a few minutes before taking a couple of pain relief pills. It was going to be a long night.

 **Amelia**

Watching Uncle Nick walk up the steps to the porch and knock on the door, I could feel my heart jump with every knock. Doubt settled in as it repeated in my head how much I didn't want this dinner. I wasn't ready for it. I wasn't ready to see Henry, Lany, and Asher. I wasn't ready to be ignored by Drake. Did it matter that Lindsay wasn't going to be there? He became so angry when I was around his brothers earlier. At the third knocking sound, the door swung open to reveal Mable in her bright yellow apron and flowy red sundress. "Come in, Come in!" Mable smiled brightly, quickly grabbing my uncle by his arm and waving for me to follow.

I could smell before I saw a roast sitting on the table, Landon setting out the bowl of roasted potatoes, and another with the roasted carrots. "Evening, Darlin'." Asher came up from behind me, wrapping me in a hug. How could his touch soothe me yet put me so on edge? His embrace warmed my heart, but my mind kept me at a distance. Henry walked in with napkins while Lany left to grab more sides.

The blonde looked at me and tilted his head. "What's wrong?"

Asher turned me around at his brother's words to look me up and down to make sure I was physically alright. "Are you okay?" Asher asked me before looking at his brother, concern in his eyes. Were my eyes red? I hadn't looked in a mirror recently, but I also hadn't cried for the past hour or so. Were my eyes still puffy?

"I'm okay." I lied, shrugging Asher off.

"Did something happen between you and Drake?" Henry asked, walking over.

"Did he say something to hurt you?" Asher and Henry's protectiveness showing through. I could see the flashes of anger at the thought of me getting hurt in their eyes. They didn't care if it was their brother; they didn't care about Drake's alpha abilities. If I were a betting woman, I would wager the three younger Windsor boys' urge to hurt Drake at my tears would outweigh any alpha presence. Lany came back in with a plate of asparagus and broccoli. "Is that why you didn't come back with him?"

I shook my head; I couldn't be bombarded with these questions. I couldn't have them acting as if they cared so much about me. "Let's have a nice supper, shall we?" Mable asked as she and my uncle came into the dining room.

As if the universe wanted to fuck with me more, Drake walked in and looked up at me, no recognition in his eyes. Asher left my side and went to Uncle Nick. "It's good to have you back, Sir. I can't say it enough." Asher gave him a quick hug, both of them patting the other's back before separating.

"Good evening, Drake." Uncle Nick smiled at the alpha, and I looked between them to see what would happen. Drake nodded and walked over, shaking Uncle Nick's hand.

"Evening…" His voice trailed off as if searching for a name before clearing his throat. "Sir, it's nice to meet you." Silence fell over the room, everyone looking at Drake as if he'd grown a third eye.

"Drake." My voice was soft and hesitant, not knowing how he would act towards me. He'd have to, at the very least, acknowledge my existence with so many people around.

"Good evenin', ma'am." He nodded, smiling in greeting before walking over, putting his hand out to shake my hand. This was wrong, all wrong. Drake wasn't being rude, but why did he act as if we were meeting for the first time? Did he want to simply restart and have a fresh beginning? I stared at his hand for what felt like forever. Drake cleared his throat again before putting his hand down and putting it in his pocket.

I sat between Henry and Asher while Lany and Drake sat across from us with Mable and Uncle Nick at each end. We held hands while Uncle Nick said grace before passing the food around the table, and putting what we wanted on our plates. "Are we going to talk about what happened?" Henry asked, jumping straight to the point.

"Happened with What?" Drake asked, looking lost.

"Between you two." Landon gestured between Drake and me with his fork.

"Her? Nothing." Drake shook his head as if his brother were talking nonsense.

The heat of rage gathered in my chest at his words. Nothing? Me, crying, in his arms after he told me of his brother's

66

betrayal was nothing to him? I stood and slammed my fist on the wooden table. "No, Drake. I want to know. What the fuck is going on?" He looked about to speak, but I put a hand up to silence him. This alpha needed to listen. "I want to know why. Why did you give me the cold shoulder and then suddenly act as if I'm your world when we were alone? And now? Now you're acting as if we've never even met before!" I couldn't help the voice crack in my words. Tears stung my eyes, and I couldn't tell if they were from sadness or anger. Either way, I did not want him to see my tears.

"What are you talking about?" His eyebrows raised, his eyes glancing at his brothers beside me, who both started to try and soothe me by putting a hand on my arm. "We have never been alone." He looked around the table to reassure everyone, defending his honor as if to say he would never cheat on his fiancée. His lies stung and took the air from me. "Look, you might be new here, but let me clue you into what goes on 'round here. You have no ground to stand on with me, and you might have my brother's attraction, but you won't have mine. Lying won't get you anywhere either, so just sit your sorry ass down and enjoy the meal my mother made you." He bared his fangs to intimidate me. I could also feel the power behind his words. Although I tried fighting it, I sat down while I continued my questioning.

The three other brothers glared at Drake. "Do you seriously not remember anything on patrol this morning? Nothing about how they," I pointed at the three other Windsor Boys in the room, "betrayed me? Absolutely nothing about holding me as I cried after you told me? What about me need-ing to stay near you?"

Drake looked me up and down, narrowing his eyes. "You have been spying on me. I didn't do that to you. I did that to Amelia, my fiancée."

I blinked, completely silenced at his words. Taking a few extra seconds to process what he had said. There was the sound of coughing as Landon took of bite of his food when Drake spoke, the food going down the wrong pipe. This only confirmed in my mind, I wasn't hallucinating. He really said my name, but wasn't referring to me. Did he realize he said my name and not Lindsay's? "Drake." I took a deep breath, not knowing if I wanted to know the answer to my next ques-tion. "Who do you think I am?" I asked slowly.

"You're my brother's whore. You probably found out we all were in love with the same woman and shared her until she disappeared. You hoped it would happen to you, too. Proba-bly some low-life gold digger. News flash, I'm engaged to the woman whom my brothers disowned."

Once again, the room was silent enough to hear a pin drop. "You're wrong." Henry was the one to break the silence after a few long moments. Everyone looked at him, and real-ization dawned on Henry's face. "That does explain all of it. Ever since you met Lindsay, you've changed."

"Who the fuck is Lindsay? Is it you?" Drake glared at me, accusingly.

"Drake." Uncle Nick calmly leaned forward. "When did Amelia come back?"

"A couple of months after she disappeared. We came back from searching for her one night and went into town for a food run. I found her in the grocery store. She seemed scared. She couldn't even afford a bag of chips."

"Drake, that wasn't Amelia. It was Lindsay." Henry spoke cautiously. Drake's energy radiated with tension.

"You're lying." Drake seethed. "I found Amelia. You three disowned her." He looked at Mable. "You grew to hate her, too."

I looked at my uncle, seething more with every word the alpha spoke. "I'm going to cut a bitch." My seat scooted back slightly as I backed up from the table. I didn't know where she was, but to Hell if I wasn't going to find her.

"You will not harm my mate," Drake growled as he too stood and stepped back.

"*You* already have." I snapped back before leaving the dining room and storming out of the house, running as soon as the front door closed behind me.

Her family owned a shop in town. What kind? Fuck, what kind of shop? I raked through my memories of the cunt and remembered her talking about a bakery. I'd tear every bakery to shreds, not caring what got fucked up so long as I killed her. I hadn't run far when it felt like a truck slammed me to the ground. "You will NOT harm her." Drake's alpha words ran through my nerves, causing my body to want to stop. It was mind over matter, though. I was not going to give in. There was too much anger in my blood right now.

Pushing him off me, we both stood quickly. "She is not who you think she is!" I yelled. I could feel my claws start shifting. I would fight this man if it meant he'd listen to reason. The bitch needed to die. "Have you ever seen her shift? Is Lindsay even a fucking dragon?!"

"Of course I've seen her shift." His movements paused for a split second. "Wait, you know about dragons?"

"I am a fucking dragon! I lived down the road from you forever!" I pointed in the direction from which we came. "I fell in love with you and your brothers. I fucked Asher first, infuriating you that he got to me before you could. You wanted to wait until I was a little older, but threw those thoughts away as soon as Asher carved that date into his door. Then I had you, Landon, and then Henry last." Angry and desperate tears threatened to spill as I yelled at the man whose malice slowly turned into confusion. "Look, I don't care if you don't love me anymore." I lied. "But I'll be damned if you think you love someone else because you believe they are me." That was the breaking point. I let the tears fall as I glared at him and turned, walking towards the city again.

"Hey," Drake said, sounding ashamed. "Hey!" He called again, seeing I still wasn't listening to him. I heard an exasperated sigh before, "Amelia." My name didn't sound right, sounding foreign when he said it, causing me to stop. I didn't look back, hearing his footsteps getting closer. "I don't know if you're telling the truth or not, but I also don't know how you'd know all those things without a good explanation. Why don't we head back to my place to talk this out? My mother would be upset if we let the food get cold."

I looked into the alpha's eyes and nodded, unable to say no to his reasoning. I also couldn't hide the fact that my stomach was yelling at me for not eating since breakfast. "Fine." We walked side by side back to the manor, both standing tall and unyielding in trying to make the other feel small. Drake was only allowed to do that if I first agreed to it, and with how he was acting, I wasn't going to give him that much power over me yet.

By the time we got back to the Windsor Manor, Uncle Nick had the three younger Windsors enthralled by a story of me, him, and my Aunt Carol having fought a set of dragon hunters back in Arizona. Mable was busy making sure the food didn't get cold. Nick stopped his story when we walked back into the room. "I'll finish the story later." He winked at the boys.

"I need answers." Drake demanded, "And if she's Amelia, that would make you Nick, and you'd know all of the answers I need." Uncle Nick nodded, gesturing for everyone to sit down again. Mable smiled as everyone sat and started to gather food back on their plate. "First, why don't I see her as Amelia? Why have I seen… Lindsay?… As Amelia?" The name Lindsay also sounded foreign coming from him.

Uncle Nick sighed and shook his head. "I'd hoped everything would be dealt with by the time we got back. Things were reported to have been taken care of by one of my cousins." He looked at me. "The reason we left is because we were found by a coven, the Sliver of Divinity. It was supposedly the same coven that killed your parents, my sister."

"The same ones that killed…" My soft voice trailed off as I slowly moved my hand comfortingly across my abdomen.

"Kind of," Nick said, ignoring the questioning glances everyone gave me. "Same coven, different sector. Anyway," He was quick to change back to the reason we left, rather than how I had lost my child. I couldn't express at the moment how appreciative I was for it. That was my story to tell when I was ready to tell it. "I suspected something was off and contacted your grandfather. He sent out a few spies. They confirmed the coven had moved in and were eyeing us. The afternoon before we left, while you were hanging out with the boys, one tried to break into the house. There was no question in my mind; we had to leave immediately. I had no worries about you guys. I knew the coven was only after our family and had been for generations. I didn't think they would have influenced you or anyone else around here after we left no trace of where we disappeared to. Unfortunately, it seems they got to one of you." He looked at Drake. "I'll ask my father if he knows of anyone who could help cure your magically inclined ailment. I also need to know more about this Lindsay person to see if she is part of the Sliver of Divinity." It's possible she is part of another coven against dragons, since there are a few out there.

Drake crossed his arms. "Why didn't you just tell us why you were leaving? Why not tell us where you were going?"

Nick sighed again. "I thought, if you didn't know where we were, then they would leave your family alone. They have ways of gaining memories from people."

"We could have helped! We could have stopped them!" Drake started to yell.

"This is no *new* questioning, Drake!" I yelled back. "I've told and asked him everything you're saying and more! I can't tell you how many times I begged him to let me come back." Tears freely fell from my eyes. "How many nights I cried myself to sleep because I lost the only thing that I had left of you guys." Henry rubbed my arm, trying to ease my pain.

"It's okay. You're here now." Henry whispered, though everyone in the room could hear him. "You won't have to leave again." He looked at Nick for reassurance. With a nod of confirmation, Henry put his arm around me as I turned and cried into his shoulder.

"I'm sorry." My shoulders shook while I tried taking deep breaths to stop crying, but it was no use. I thought I'd cried all my tears earlier today. How can one person cry so much in one day?

"You have nothing to be sorry about," Henry spoke against my hair and kissed the top of my head.

I did, though; I lost the baby. I lost the one thing they'd given me to keep and nourish, and I wasn't able to tell them yet. The words weren't able to come out. All I was able to say was "I'm so sorry."

Chapter Five

Wednesday, October 4th, 2017

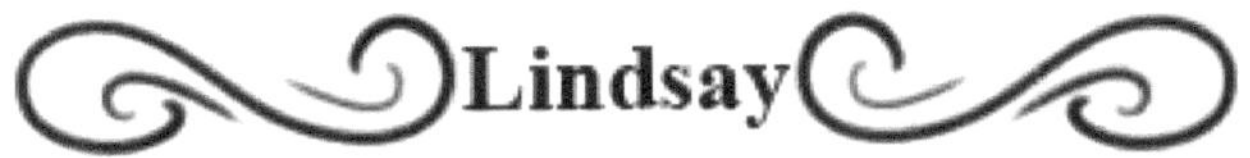

LINDSAY STOMPED DOWN THE STAIRS FROM HER room, grumbling to herself. She hadn't gotten much sleep last night, having grown accustomed to sleeping next to Drake. "That stupid bitch. I swear I'm going to curse her very existence." She slumped into a seat at the small dining table while her ditz of a mother cooked eggs.

"Oh, honey, I didn't realize you were going to be home this morning." As always, her mother was chirpier than what was normal for the early hours of Sun. "Would you like me to make you breakfast too? I am just about done making your father's."

"I'll eat later." Lindsay rolled her eyes. She had worse problems than breakfast.

"Aww, are you okay?" Trudy put the pan down and leaned over the counter to listen to her daughter.

"Yes. I'm fan -fucking- tastic, mom." Lindsay glared up at the brunette. "Two years. Two damned years I've been trying to get that alpha without raising suspicion, I finally get him to propose and then, two weeks later, some heifer shows up out of nowhere and is challenging me for him."

Lindsay's father looked up from the paperwork that was sprawled out on his desk in front of him to his daughter. "What did you say?" He stood up and walked across the living room to the small dining area. When her father joined the conversation, her mother went back to finishing up cooking breakfast.

"You know damn well what I said."

Al stood over her and backhanded Lindsay, causing her head to whip to the side. "Don't you dare talk to me that way. I am your father. You will show me respect." He caressed the cheek that was quickly turning pink. His face softened as if he hadn't just hit his daughter. "My sweet honey, if you only acted like a lady and treated me with the respect I deserve as your father, I wouldn't have to do that. Your actions have consequences." He pulled out a chair for himself to sit next to her. "Now, tell me about the girl who appeared."

"Her name is Amelia. She was there with Mable the other day, and the brothers practically fawned over her. I had to fight with Drake's memories to quickly warp his vision of her. Once he saw her, I started losing his connection."

Al smirked. "Did she say if she came alone?"

"I don't know. She spent the night at the Windsor's Manor. She probably came alone and had nowhere to stay." Lindsay raked her memories trying to think.

"No, she has a place to stay. She always has had a place to stay." Al gritted through his teeth. "I can't get close to her damned house without their wards sucking the magic from my fingertips." He held his palms up, wiggling his fingers. "No wands, stones, or books have been able to get close either without losing their magic. The closest I've gotten is the dirt road leading up to the Swallow's cabin. The last time anyone got close enough to recon was when we hired a non-magic user to scout it out." His voice kept getting softer as he spoke and looked up from his hands. "She's the dragon who got your cousin Nathanial killed in Arizona."

Lindsay's eye twitched at the new knowledge. "I'm going to kill her." She pushed her chair back as she went to stand, but was quickly forced back down by her father's hand on her shoulder.

He chuckled. "You think you're getting past the other brothers to get to her when you can't even keep Drake from canceling dinner with you?" her father smirked, remembering the small rampage she'd had last night on her way up to and in her room. "You have a lot to learn about this girl before you make your move. You also need to learn if she came back alone or not. This is *very* important information." He squeezed her shoulder a little too tightly for emphasis.

"Yes, sir." She looked down.

"I will be calling Amber and having her family come to town." Rage burned in Lindsay's chest, knowing who all would be coming from that family. She quickly plastered a fake smile on her face to appease her father. Amber Barlough was the woman her father had always been in love with. If it weren't for the woman's inability to reproduce, she'd probably be Lindsay's mother. Instead, Amber and Alvin kept pushing Amber's stepson, Douglas, onto her. Douglas wasn't of any help either, playing their parents' game and pursuing Lindsay anytime they were together. He was a charmer, sure, but he always had a way to make Lindsay feel inferior. Thankfully, she had Drake, her fiancé, as an excuse to deny Douglas's advances.

Why would her father call the Barloughs anyway? It wasn't like this was something she couldn't do on her own. She was so close to finishing her personal mission of getting Drake anyway. What was one bitch in the mix? There had to be something her father wasn't telling her. "Now, you need to go and find out anything and everything you can about Amelia. Report back to me once you find out if she came back alone or not.

"Who would she have come back with? I didn't see anyone else with her. She didn't mention anything about anyone."

"We need to know who all we are up against." Alvin stood up and walked back to his desk before pointing to the door. "Go. Now." Lindsay muttered curses as she walked out of the house, electricity jumping from finger to finger as she did so. If Lindsay had any say in the matter, Amelia was not only going to die, but she was going to suffer.

Amelia

The even sound of breathing was the first thing I registered as consciousness pulled me away from my dreamless sleep. Next was the pressure on my abdomen and around my thigh. Peaking open an eye, I leaned my head up to see the blonde of Henry's head on my stomach and his arm around my leg. The three younger Windsor boys and I had decided to stay over at my house after dinner while Drake opted to stay at the Windsors, saying he needed to think and work through a few things.

I could hear the muffled voices of Uncle Nick, Lany, and Drake downstairs due to my door being slightly ajar. Asher was probably out on patrol. My hand traveled into the soft blonde hair as I thought about the night prior. Things had died down, and not much yelling happened after my uncle finally let out the reason we left. It was stupid, but I could also see why he did it, thinking about my safety. I truly believed that, if he knew I was pregnant at the time, he would have at least talked it out with my boys before taking me away. They could have come with, after some arrangements. Thinking of what-ifs would get me nowhere, no matter how many came to mind.

Henry shifted and groaned as he started to wake, squeezing my leg slightly. "Good morning, Love." He kissed my stomach, causing my breath to hitch as I pictured him doing the same to my slightly swollen belly. How he would have coddled me as I grew the little one in me. Though I didn't know which of the four was the biological father of our baby, I knew all of them would treat it as their own, loving the child no matter what. "Are you okay?" Henry asked, looking up at me as he felt my unsteady breaths.

"I'll be fine." Though my smile wasn't forced, it hid so much pain.

"If something is wrong, you know you can tell me. Right?" He sat up and moved closer to me, kissing my cheek. His hand moved a strand of hair from my face. "I want to be able to help."

I couldn't take it anymore, not with how this caring man looked at me with those unknowing eyes. I couldn't lie to him. My throat started closing as I choked on my words. Hiding my face in his chest, I let it out. "You can't help." Tears fell as I whispered. "No one can."

Henry moved me so I sat on his lap, rocking me back and forth. His hand gently rubbed my back in reassurance. "Sometimes talking about it helps."

I knew he was telling the truth. I looked up at him and then at the door that was still cracked open. I was sure the men downstairs could hear my sobs, and I didn't need them

80

to hear what I needed to say yet. "Could you close the door?" I whispered, and he nodded, getting up to close the door before coming back, holding me in his arms again. His gentle, reassuring, and calming kisses helped only slightly, as the scars I had from this story were more than just physical.

I took deep breaths, doing my best to get to a state of mind where I could talk about it, but it was taking longer than it should. The words of the nurse still echo in my head. The steady beep of the heart rate machine haunted my dreams. Henry rubbed my arms, kissing the top of my head. "Take all the time you need." Was it time I needed? Time didn't help in the past two years. I truly stopped believing people when they said time heals all wounds. How much time? They never specified, and I was never a particularly patient person.

"It's been almost two years." My voice was hoarse, so I cleared my throat, but it didn't help much.

"It's been rough on all of us, I understand." I appreciated him trying to sympathize, but he didn't understand. Not yet.

"You don't, though." I turned my head into his chest again to muffle my words. "I was pregnant." More sobs escaped me and fell onto his bare chest. I hated the word was. "I lost it. I lost my baby." And there it was, the truth, out for one of them to hear. He held me tighter, seemingly trying to process the bombshell I dropped on him.

"I…" Looking up at him, wiping the streaming tears from my eyes, I could see so many emotions flashing through his own. Anger, betrayal, grief, denial. "I'm sorry." He whispered and tightened his grip. "It's okay to cry." His words weren't what I expected, completely countering what the nurse told me. I let him process, holding him as he cried. He deserved to mourn. Whether it was his or not, Henry also lost a baby that day.

I recounted the car crash in vague detail, not being able to actually recall much of the actual crash. I hit my head too many times in the attack to remember anything more than my aunt calling out my name unless I was trapped in a panic attack or flashback. It was the hospital I remember the most.

~*~ ~*~ ~*~ ~*~ ~*~

A consistent beep was the only thing I heard around me as I began to wonder where I was, trying to recall what happened to me last. I tried to sit up, but my body wouldn't move. Opening my eyes, all I could see was white before my vision started to clear. The beeping caused my head to turn, and I could see a monitor with a heartbeat. One heartbeat. I watched and listened as the monitor showed my heart rate increase. Why was there only one? A dirty blonde woman walked into the room with a clipboard, looking through the papers on it. "Oh, you're awake." She said, looking up at me. "How are you feeling?" The nurse moved my bed to a sitting position. I was able to see all the tubes and wires across my body, a tiny mechanism on my left finger. Another beep made me glare at the monitor showing the one heartbeat.

"How is my baby?" My right arm wanted to move to my abdomen, but a cast prevented me from moving. I could see another cast on my left leg. Bruises and small cuts littered my left arm.

82

"You were in a car accident, Miss Swallow." The nurse checked my vitals and wrote things on her paper. Her voice sounded dead, bored, and unapologetically disinterested in how I was feeling. "Does anything hurt?" Like she cared.

Everything hurt, but nothing mattered until I knew my baby was alright. "Is my baby okay?" Terror boiled in my throat as I looked around, unable to see anything that showed any sign of my baby's well-being.

"Calm down, Miss Swallow. I need to know, does anything hurt? On a scale of one to ten, how bad is your pain?" She took a flashlight, blinding me as she looked into my eyes. Did the bitch not hear me? Why wasn't she telling me about my child? I mentally sent healing thoughts to my baby. Everything will be okay.

"Why won't you tell me about my baby?" My voice cracked as the beeping of the heart rate monitor sped up.

"You don't have one. There's nothing to update you on, nothing to talk about." The world stopped. I don't have one? No. I have one. I was just going to my doctor to see if it was a boy or girl. I lost my baby. The truth spoke to me through the beeps on the heart rate monitor. I've heard my baby's heartbeat before. I knew they had one, yet I could only see the one heartbeat. My heartbeat. My unbroken arm went to my abdomen, and I could feel a bandage.

"My baby." I started to cry before the nurse looked at me with disgust.

"Stop crying. It's not worth crying over. You can always have another, or you can adopt. Do you know how many children are up for adoption? Children who need a parent? I saw the dad isn't in the picture either, maybe this is for the better. You don't want to raise a fatherless child."

Throughout her lecture, I stopped crying, wanting to strangle this woman. I lost the only thing connecting me to my boys, the one thing my boys unknowingly gave me to keep safe, and I lost it.

~*~ ~*~ ~*~ ~*~~*~

"She was wrong," Henry whispered against my forehead. "We lost something special." As if something shifted, I no longer felt alone in all of this. Someone else knew exactly how I felt. The family around me did their best to comfort me, to sympathize with how they lost their sister, my mother. My grandfather was the only one who could sympathize with me the most. It was his daughter he lost. There was a difference, though, a thin wall that separated him from knowing my loss. Grandpa Harold was able to get to know the person my mother was. I didn't get the chance to even fantasize about what my boy or girl would grow up to be.

Henry, on the other hand, knew exactly the pain I'd been tormented with for the past two years. "I hope she was fired." The anger in Henry's voice was uncharacteristic. He always saw the good in everything.

"Thank you," I whispered back. "I'll tell the others, but I have to do it on my time. I know they deserve to know, but I," my voice broke, "Not now. Promise me you'll let me tell them."

"I promise." He kissed my head again, and I looked up at him, grateful for all of his understanding. I truly couldn't have asked for better men.

After several minutes of silence, holding each other, Henry helped me clean up and get ready for the day. "How do I look?" I gave him a little twirl, hoping my eyes weren't too puffy.

"You look amazing as always." He walked up to me, putting his arms around my waist. "Are you ready?"

"Yeah, I'm feeling better now." I walked downstairs with him following me to see Uncle Nick, Drake, and Lany sitting at the small breakfast table in the kitchen. Simultaneously, they all looked up at me, and I could tell by the looks in their eyes that they knew I had been crying despite the effort I put into hiding it. Lany looked at his brother behind me and then nodded, satisfied with the unspoken conversation they had. "Good morning." I smiled and went to the fridge to get milk for cereal as if I hadn't broken down, reliving my trauma. My eyes lingered on Drake's after I turned around. "Any progress?" I asked, hopeful.

"You look different, sound different too. Your hair is shorter." He made a gesture with his hands just under his ears. "It's a light brown, maybe a dirty blonde." Drake then looked at Uncle Nick. "He looks the same, but you look like a completely different person. His description of me was inaccurate at best, my dark brown hair stopping at my mid-back.

The more he spoke, the less hope I had. "I guess not," I mumbled, and Henry poured my cereal before grabbing the milk from my hand and pouring it into the bowl. I smiled as the bowl was slid back in front of me with a spoon in it.

"I called my dad this morning." Uncle Nick spoke up. "Grandpa Harold said he'd get back to me after making a few calls of his own." Uncle Nick looked at the younger men in the room. "He has more experience fighting the more… unnatural kinds of magics." Magic was one of the things I couldn't seem to get attuned to. Uncle Nick was the opposite. He was more attuned to nature than I'd ever be. It was all because of him that the forest hid our cabin from outsiders. According to him, the unnatural magic was blocked entirely from our property due to the wards he and my parents put up here. It wasn't until I was in Arizona when I learned that druidic magic was something he and my dad bonded over. "While we wait to hear back, it would be a good idea for Drake to stay here. She won't be able to come onto this property, and hopefully, the longer he stays away from Lindsay, the less of an effect her magic will have on him.

Drake shook his head, glaring at his words. "I have to talk with her. For all I know, it's you two who are playing tricks on my family, and I need to protect them.

"Would you mind if I were there with you when you talk with her?" Uncle Nick leaned back in his chair thoughtfully.

"Do you think she'll answer honestly if you're around?" Henry asked.

"Do you think she'll answer honestly at all?" I scoffed. "I say we all go talk to the bitch, and if she doesn't comply, I start breaking bones." It truly was the least I should do.

86

Drake growled, standing up, causing Lany and Henry to get between him and me. "I told you, you're not going to harm her."

I wasn't backing down at his nonverbal challenge. Daring to take a step forward, I glare at him. "And I told you, I'm going to kill her!" My fingers on the counter turned to claws as my anger controlled me.

Henry put his arms up to his shoulders and then lowered them slowly. "Let's take a deep breath." He looked at his brother. "I don't think it's a good idea for you to talk to her *alone*," he looked between the two of us, "because she would influence you further. If one or all of us are there too, we could prove she's messing with you."

"Fine," Drake growled unhappily, but agreed with his brother's reasoning. I watched him pull out his phone and call Lindsay, inviting her over to the Windsor manor. My blood boiled as he spoke to her. She didn't deserve his loving tone. He didn't love her; she only made him think he loved her.

I decided to run with Henry back to the Windsor's while Drake, Lany, and Uncle Nick drove over in the rental. On the way there, I saw Asher's dragon coming from the sky, and he landed just behind the mansion, shifting back into his human form. I stopped at the porch, taking a few extra seconds to admire his body before he put a pair of basketball shorts on. He was toned before I disappeared to Arizona, now he was built like an old Greek god, much like the other three had filled out. "Hey, Beautiful." Asher walked up and kissed my forehead. "What's she doing here?" The anger in his voice caused me to look around, making sure he wasn't talking about me.

A neon pink Mini Cooper blasting some new pop song stopped next to Henry's 1997 F250. I watched as Drake quickly got between the car and me. "Good morning, handsome." Lindsay waved as she got out of her vehicle. "I missed you last night." She looked me up and down before smiling and kissing Drake. It didn't help when he eagerly returned her kiss, pinning her to the car.

I walked into the house, unable to watch. The younger three Windsors followed me, and I sat on Lany's lap with Henry next to me and Asher sitting on the armrest of the loveseat. There was no way I'd have Drake and Lindsay sitting so close together without anyone next to them. Drake and Lindsay walked in with Uncle Nick closing the door behind him.

"Oh, you're staying out here?" Lindsay asked as she looked at me, holding Drake's hand, and went to sit on the couch. It was Uncle Nick who cleared his throat. "I'm sorry. I don't think we've met yet." Drake sat while Lindsay turned to greet my uncle. She put her hand out for a handshake, and I watched her like a hawk. Uncle Nick smiled and shook her hand, his ring emitting a faint purple glow. "My name is Lindsay. Yours?" She spoke after a few moments of silence.

"You can just call me Nick."

Lindsay let out a little yelp before pulling her hand away and checking her palm. Nick winked at me before Lindsay looked up at him. "My apologies, ma'am. My ring heats up sometimes."

"Must have something to do with the heat our hands made during the handshake." She nervously chuckled. After a reassuring squeeze from Drake, Lindsay smiled. "So, how do you two know each other?" She sat on the couch next to Drake, and Uncle Nick sat on the other side. How could he let her sit next to Drake?

"We go way back, but it's been a while since I've been able to visit. I thought it might be good to catch up. How do you know Drake?"

"We're engaged." Lindsay's eyes lit up at the excuse to show off the expensive ring. She held out her hand to show it off, glancing at me before looking back at my uncle, who leaned forward to examine the massive diamonds.

"Congratulations. How did you two meet?" Nick leaned back, looking more relaxed. What about her ring made him so at ease?

"Well," Drake said, looking lovingly at Lindsay. "You could say we were child-" He cut off his sentence when Lindsay touched his knee. "We were like children when we met." He corrected his slip. My eyes were drawn to the purple sparkle of her fingernails.

"I felt like an elementary school kid with her first crush." Lindsay giggled, causing me to gag. "Shut it bitch. Just because he loves me, doesn't mean you can act like that." I rolled my eyes, my hand squeezing Lany's arm tighter. Lindsay was only one mage. We were 6 dragons; we could take her on. But then again, Drake would fight on the mage's side, and it would be a tougher fight with him being an alpha.

"You know what they say, love is blind." Uncle Nick smiled at the two. I couldn't act like I was okay with this. How could my uncle be such a good actor? What did he know that I didn't?

"And hindsight is 2020," I coldly added to the saying.

"Look bitch, I'm trying to be nice and civil. At the very least, you could try to do the same." Lindsay cleared her throat and took a breath. "I'm sorry that we got off on the wrong foot."

"She's not worth you getting upset over." Drake rolled his eyes and gave me a look as if to say, "Grow up."

"That's it!" I yelled, getting off Lany, but as soon as I stood up, so did everyone else. Between Lindsay and me stood Drake, Henry, Landon, Asher, and Nick in that order, with Nick pushing me back and completely body-blocking me. "Call off your spells," I growled.

"I don't know what you're talking about." Lindsay sighed, looking at her nails.

"Your mind tricks. I know he sees you as if you were me. I know when he sees me, you've distorted his vision. Call them off and let's see how he truly feels." Pressure in my head grew as I felt horns curling out from my temples towards my face. My fingers turned to claws, and black scales started to form on my hands, up my forearms, and my vision flashed red.

"Honey, you have so much to learn," Lindsay tisked. "I'm not going to call it off. I've worked too damn hard for too damn long for it all to just crumble because some skank showed up to ruin it." She spoke through her teeth with hands fisted at her side. Sparks of electricity danced around the mage's wrists.

"Tell me, what coven do you hold allegiance to?" Nick asked.

"I don't know who you are to be asking. I assume you're with the bitch." Lindsay glared. "It shouldn't matter to you."

Drake looked back at Lindsay. "You're a mage?"

"Oh, you won't remember that, Sweetheart, but for now, I'll let you think on it. Not like you'll be able to do anything about it when I come back." She snapped her fingers, and smoke flooded the room, only dispersing after I heard the front door slam shut and the sound of her car speeding down the road.

"Fuck! Where does she live?" I stomped towards the door. "I'll gut her like a fish! I'll tear her limbs off and beat her with 'em. I'll break every Goddamned bone in her body." With every sentence, Drake's growls got louder.

"Enough!" His alpha-infused roar caused me to pause. "Look, I'm confused and not getting answers. Killing her won't do anything helpful. Does anyone have any good, *helpful* ideas?"

Uncle Nick cleared his throat, causing the room to turn to him. "I might not know the most about their kinds of magic, but I do know the safest place for you, Drake, is at our cabin."

"Then why was he still under her spell when he was over earlier?" I questioned. It had been bothering me since I left the cabin.

"That magic has changed his memory. I don't believe it to be an ongoing spell, and thus the magic doesn't dissipate when he walks through the boundaries."

"We need the fucking specialist," I muttered, walking out the door. Drake quickly followed after to make sure I wasn't going to go out and harm his *future mate*. "I'm going to shift," I called out, not bothering to take off my clothes as they ripped at the shift in my size. I flew close to the top tree line towards the lake. It felt like a weight was lifted off my shoulders, for even just a temporary time, as I let my wings spread. If only for these short few minutes, everything in the world felt right and I had no problems. Upon realizing it was Wednesday, and the boat tours would be out soon, I flew up, so I was hidden by the clouds. From up here, I had no care in the world. Everything on the ground could wait until I was good and ready to deal with it. After a couple of minutes of the only sound being the wind, other sets of wings flapped around me.

"Lia!" Lany mentally called out. Telepathy was a handy ability when we were all shifted. Giggling to myself, I dove into one of the fluffier clouds. The feeling of cold water droplets soothed my scales. "Come out, come out, wherever you are!" The red dragon chimed.

I mentally smiled at how, in the air, I could act as if nothing of the past two years had happened. "You gotta be quicker than that." I watched as the clouds moved, signaling how Henry and Lany were flying around. They were never good at being discreet in the clouds.

 **Drake**

On the ground, Drake shook his head, standing next to Nick, looking at the sky. "Will you give me the answers I'm looking for?" He remembered how he felt when Amelia had first disappeared, confused, lost, and hurt. All of those emotions came back tenfold.

"I don't think I can, but I will do my damndest to try and help in any way I can."

"When will we hear back from your father?"

"Once he's been able to contact someone, he'll call me." A small buzzing came from Nick's pocket, and as he pulled his phone out, the older man chuckled. "Speak of the devil and he shall appear. I better take this."

Asher put his hand on his brother's shoulder. "I'll help you pack if you need."

"I just need a couple sets of clothes and my laptop." Drake sighed as he watched the clouds. "Idiots, they never were good at finding her up there." Although his mind and recollection were telling him it wasn't Amelia up there, after what he heard the woman, whom he thought was Amelia, say, he started to question everything.

Asher chuckled. "Yeah, I know why I could always find her," he pointed to his nose, hinting at his heightened sense of smell, "but I never could understand how you did."

Drake pointed to the clouds. "I learned how she moves without disturbing the clouds much. She likes bigger clouds because there's more hiding space, but if there is none, she tends to hide just above the bottom of the clouds."

"I never realized that." Asher smiled up before heading back inside, his oldest brother following him. Drake rubbed his temple, feeling the onset of another headache.

Amelia

I laughed as Lany once again passed me, causing the clouds to shift and me to subsequently move in order to stay undetected. "Come on! You're not even trying!" The best part about telepathy, while shifted, is that it sounded like a voice in your head and didn't come from any direction. Playfully, I jumped from my position as he came around, passing me again, causing us to fall below the clouds.

"Fuck!" Lany yelled out of surprise, looking back at me. "Lia, what if they saw us?" It was a serious question, but I couldn't help but laugh.

"Fuck 'em." I dove downward, both Henry and Lany following me, and did a flip before landing in the lake. I shifted back into my human form to swim back to shore, where an old, torn-down building once was. The only thing left of it was the concrete pillars and foundation. I remember it being

94

a park and lodge that sat on the water, but had become unstable, and was torn down for the most part. Looking over at the abandoned tennis court, I observed the holes in the surrounding fence. "This place sure has changed." I walked to one of our bins disguised as a trash can and removed the side to reveal the clothes we had hidden inside. I put on one of their old button-up shirts that came down to my mid-thigh. Before I could button the shirt, though, Landon stopped me, putting a hand on my lower abdomen.

"What?" I nervously looked up at him.

The redhead traced the light line of my scar, making my skin shudder at how tenderly he touched me. "New scar?" Fuck, I wasn't ready to have this conversation so soon again.

Henry put his hand on his brother's shoulder. "A battle scar of a long and grueling war."

"Was this from when they attacked you back in Arizona?" Landon looked at me, concerned, before pulling me against him in a tight embrace. "I won't let them lay another finger on you." He kissed my forehead and looked me in the eyes. "I won't let it happen."

"Thank you." The words were hard to get out with the lump forming in my throat. I couldn't put into words how thankful I was that Lany somehow knew I wasn't ready to talk about it and took it at face value, not asking any questions. The mark hurt more than I would like to admit. He might not understand why I had that scar, specifically, but he knew I would explain it in time.

"Anytime." He smiled brightly and let go so I could finish buttoning the shirt.

I held both of their hands after they both put on jeans, and we walked into town. "If Drake is staying at your place, where is he going to be staying? I mean, he wouldn't be sleeping with us because he's still processing everything. You don't necessarily have a guest bedroom." Looking up at Henry as he thought out loud, I couldn't help but feel hurt at the realization. I knew it would take time, even if the truth of the matter was shoved in Drake's face earlier.

"I think the couch in the living room is a pull-out." It wasn't an issue in the past; they all usually slept in the living room after a movie night together, or they all slept at the Windsor's. The cabin wasn't big, but it wasn't small either, a simple two-bed, three-bath with a living room, kitchen, dining room, and a little reading area at the back door. "You guys will stay, though, right?" I stopped walking at a realization and looked at both men beside me. "What about your mother? I don't want anything happening to Mable."

"We'll figure it out and talk with her after she gets off work." Lany tried to comfort me with a reassuring smile. We emerged from the tree line onto the road and gave a little wave to each vehicle as they passed by. There were a few of them who recognized who I was, waving a bit more enthusiastically as a greeting.

"We should give her a visit, keeping her updated just in case Lindsay shows up at the visitor center and tries something." I walk faster with my new mission in mind. I wouldn't have another person I love influenced by that mage.

 **Drake**

The eldest and youngest of the Windsor brothers, along with Nick, arrived at the cabin and unloaded what was all packed. "I'm sorry, this is all we have for you right now." Nick went to the couch and removed the cushions to make the couch into a bed.

"Why am I on the couch?" Drake's head pounded, and his body begged for unconsciousness. It did get slightly better once they arrived at the cabin and even more after the pain meds kicked in, but it was slowly getting worse again. Rubbing his temples, the alpha did his best to recall why they were forcing him to stay here. He could recall he'd been told before, but couldn't remember the reason.

"Did you want to sleep with Amelia and your brothers in her room, upstairs?" Nick's question didn't sound right, making his head hurt further.

"Never mind." Drake shook his head and helped Nick set up the couch bed.

"Don't worry, my father said he found someone who should be here within the next few days, I hope." Nick put a hand on Drake's shoulder and smiled at the confused, younger man. "Hopefully, the longer you stay here, the more things will make sense."

"Thanks, I think I just need some sleep." Drake put the blanket on the bed before falling on his face, bouncing slightly on the pull-out, and passed out as soon as his head hit the pillow.

Chapter Six

Saturday, October 7th, 2017

THREE LONG DAYS HAD PASSED SINCE THE incident. The Windsors were all living in the cabin, with three of the four men sleeping in my bed with me, Drake sleeping in the living room on the pull-out, and Mable sharing the bed with Uncle Nick. We all were cautious but went about what became our daily routine. Mable and Nick went to work, leaving early in the morning, and the brothers, apart from Drake, made their rounds in the forest and lake. Drake was put on house arrest, and I stayed at the house to watch him. I kept my distance, staying upstairs, for the most part, only coming downstairs for occasional snacks and drinks. He was already confined to the property; I didn't want to make him feel even more trapped by my presence. I could tell in the few times we did cross paths, he didn't see me as me yet, and was overly cautious when I was around.

Uncle Nick kept in touch with Grandpa Harold about the doctor who specialized in mental magics. We got updates daily, but they were inconsistent on the timeline. Some days we were told two days, some days we were told he had been held up, and it would take him a week to get to us.

Lany and I were cooking lunch while Drake had stepped out onto the front porch. I could tell as the days passed by, Drake was getting further on edge, frustration growing. Being cooped up meant he wasn't able to shift, and I knew doing so would help. The only problem was that we couldn't risk Lindsay finding him again. Who knew what she would do if she got her hands on his mind this time? "It will be alright," Lany whispered, his arm slowly wrapping around my waist. "Hopefully, the doctor will get here within the next couple of days, and he'll get the help he needs." Lany's head rested on my shoulder, comforting me with light kisses along my neck.

"I'm worried he'll explode on one of us before then." I sighed, "He's already so angry. He can't stand to be in the same room as me. He's snapped a few times at you guys already."

"It's because you're looking more and more like yourself as her magic fades." It was a lie. Drake looked at me as if I were the gum stuck to the bottom of his shoe. "He's been exposed to her magic inside his mind for almost two years.

I'm just glad he's making this much progress in just a few days." Lany stepped back and took the pot of boiling noodles off the stove, draining the water from them.

"Hearing the cunt say she messed with his mind probably helps him fight the mental battles. I wish he could let out some steam, though." I poured the sauce on the ground beef and turned the heat down to a simmer before stirring.

Landon's hands went to my hips as he whispered close to my ear. "I know how to get your mind off your worries." His words sent shivers down my spine as his hands gripped tighter and pulled me against him. I could feel his growing excitement pressing against my ass. My mind went to the alpha outside, but the thought only made my heart beat faster. We both knew Drake wouldn't come inside until I returned to my room, unable to stand being around me. "How long until Asher and Henry get back?" Lany nipped at the base of my neck, causing a soft moan to escape my lips.

Smirking, I turned around in his grasp. "I think we have enough time."

He chuckled at my excitement, and I watched his golden eyes flash with fire behind them. "That's good enough for me." He picked me up, spinning around to place me on the island countertop. His hands slowly moved up my outer thighs and beneath my skirt. "Is here okay?" He asked, grabbing my ass, moving his hips to grind against my wetness. Lany trailed kisses up my collarbone to just under my ear as he waited for my reply.

Nodding, I grabbed at his jeans and undid his belt. "Here is good." His kisses sent jolts of need to my core. He smiled against my neck, gripping the sides of my thong, and slid them down my legs, pocketing them in his back pocket. Locking eyes with him, I pulled out his half-hard cock, biting my lip as I slowly stroked it. Despite our agreement of not having too much time, we absolutely loved teasing each other, playing the game to see who would break first. Who would beg for the other? Neither of us liked being the weaker-willed in this relationship, always fighting to have the upper hand and challenging the other.

Unwilling to be outdone, Lany sucked on his first two fingers to get them wet before pushing up my skirt to rub against my sensitive nub. "Shit." He whispered as he touched my pussy, my grip on his cock tightened as heat went straight to my core. I could hear him suck in a quick breath at my grasp and I bit my lip, composure threatening to give. Every sound he made both egged me on further and caused heat to shoot straight to where his fingers ribbed me. Not wanting to be outdone, I stroked him faster and leaned forward, moaning softly in his ear. "Fuck, Lia." He whispered and moved his hips, thrusting into my hand. There'd been once or twice when we'd both gotten off only with the other's hands because neither of us begged for the fuck.

Landon moved his fingers in and out of me, but it wasn't until he moved his fingers in a come-hither motion that my brain turned off. Suddenly, his fingers weren't enough. I needed to be filled. "Lany." I whimpered, my hips moving involuntarily as my pussy pleaded for more, wanting his fingers to go deeper.

"Yes, Lia?" He spoke casually as if he wasn't breathing hard and his hard cock wasn't dripping with precum. As much as I wanted to say fuck him for being an arrogant prick, I didn't want him to stop.

"I want you in me. Now." I leaned up and kissed him deeply, wrapping my legs around him.

"All you had to do was ask, Lia." He picked me up, spinning me around, bending me over the counter. "Fuck, you're so wet." Lany groaned, tapping his length at my entrance a few times, his other hand on my hip, before he quickly thrust deep inside me.

"Holy Fuck." I moaned before biting my fist to try and help silence my moans. Immediately, his cock found every pleasure spot in me as he thrust in and out. The cool counter against my chest contrasted with the heat of his hands, the sensations mixing to increase my pleasure. My toes barely grazed the floor with each of his thrusts.

"Shit, Lia." His grip tightened as he thrust harder into me. Fuck, his moans were music to my ears, and I gripped the edge of the counter, needing something to hold onto. "Lia." He moaned, and he sounded just as close as I felt, both of us holding back for as long as we could.

"More, Lany. Please." He pulled out of me and turned me so my back was pressed against the counter. His eyes had shifted to his shining golden, slitted dragon eyes. The fire behind them burned bright as he looked me up and down. My chest heaved as I tried to catch my breath, annoyance growing when he smirked but didn't move.

Leaning down so his lips barely grazed my ear, he whispered. "What was that?" Fuck this man.

"I'll finish myself if you don't make me cum." I threaten, looking deep into his eyes.

"Come on." He gripped my hips and pressed against me, his cock hard against my abdomen. "You just need to say those words again." One of his hands went to my chin, trailing his hand on my cheek. "Three. Little. Words."

I bit my bottom lip. Fuck, I wanted this. I needed this. Why did he have to be such an asshole? "Lany," I whisper, closing my eyes, and move against him, causing him to moan at the friction. "More, please."

At my last word, Lany's lips connected with mine, and he picked me up, causing me to wrap my legs around him and his cock thrust deep in my core. I didn't muffle my moans as he fucked me against the fridge. The build up of pleasure came too quickly, as my orgasm came fast and hard. I rode it out, with my juices slowly running down his legs. "Fuck, Lia, I'm so close."

"Wait." In my dazed mind, I panicked slightly, and he stopped immediately. I could see concern cross his eyes as he looked down at me. I unwrapped my legs from him, and he let me stand, his cock sliding out of me. I went to my knees in front of him and smiled, licking my lips as I see my juices covering his cock. I moaned, licking from the base to his tip.

"Holy fuck!" His hand instinctively went to the back of my head with his fingers lacing through my hair. He thrust in my mouth, and I sucked hard, moaning around his cock. "Look at me." He panted, and I closed my eyes, focusing on making him feel as good as possible. "Lia." I wasn't going to unless he begged. He broke me, I'll break him. Moaning louder, sending more vibrations around his cock, he thrust faster. "Lia, please." My hand went to his balls, and I started playing with them, still with my eyes closed. "Please, Lia, look at me." He whimpered, and as I looked up, I locked eyes with him. "Fuck, I'm cumming." His gruff voice sent more shivers down my spine. With a few more thrusts into my mouth, his warm cum spurt into my mouth, and he gripped the fridge to stay standing. I swallowed as much as I could and got the rest that had dripped down my chin with a finger, sucking on it while meeting his gaze.

I froze as I heard tires on gravel, signaling a vehicle approaching. Looking back up at Lany, I saw the slight panic as he heard it too, his smirk faltering. I helped him as he put his cock back in his pants, and I adjusted my clothes, doing our best to act as if nothing had just happened between us. Standing, I glanced at the stove with the simmering sauce and pot of drained pasta still in the sink. I quickly washed my hands and put the pasta and sauce on hot pads on the dining table. Lany washed his hands and turned off the stove before bringing down plates from the cupboard, placing the stack on the dining table. "You'll need to get cleaned up," Lany smirked as he spanked my ass.

"Yeah, and? You will too, they will smell me all over you." I smile. It was rare that I would talk about my sexual encounters with the different Windsors. Usually, what happened behind "closed doors" stayed there, though with Lany, it was different. He was always one for a quickie, and afterward, although we would both smell like sex and the other person, no one would talk about it.

"So, you want them to be at your knees, begging for your sweet pussy instead of wanting to eat the food we just slaved over?"

"You have a point." I started walking towards the stairs when the front door opened.

Drake

Outside, Drake had to stop reading his book, unable to concentrate due to the noises behind him, inside the cabin. His grip tightened on the old, wooden rocker he sat on, aggressively tossing the book on his lap. The alpha looked back at the closed curtains, wanting more than anything to yell at his brother to keep it down or to at least have the decency to take it upstairs. He could smell the food inside, and his stomach yelled at him, not for the first time, for not having eaten breakfast. Drake knew that he couldn't leave the property, but damn was it tempting. He tried once again to focus on the book, but when he heard the woman call out his brother's name, he almost lost all self-control. Drake decided that, until his other two brothers came back, he would take a walk

106

around the border of the property. It was better than breaking any part of the house in his aggression.

Thankfully, he didn't have to wait long. As soon as Drake got to the edge of the property, Henry's F250 crossed the property line with Asher in the passenger seat. They stopped when they saw him and rolled down the window. "Hey, Bro." Henry nodded his head at Drake. "Where do you think you're going?"

"Calm down, I'm not leaving. I just needed to get as far away from that house as I could. I was just going for a walk."

"What's wrong?"

Annoyance boiled in his chest, and Drake shook his head, doing his best to remove her sounds out of his mind. "I couldn't concentrate enough to read."

"Your head?" Asher asked, leaning over the center console. It was the youngest of his brothers who assisted him on more than one occasion with getting pain meds these past few days. "Hop in?" Asher pointed to the bed of the pickup.

"I'd rather not. I'm going to walk back, hopefully it will be gone by the time y'all pull up." Drake turned and started walking to the house, leaving behind his confused brothers, who slowly followed him, concerned for their oldest brother.

"I think he's getting worse." Henry looked at Asher.

"May the doctor get here soon," Asher agreed, nodding.

Amelia

Standing in the front doorway, Henry looked me up and down while Asher took in a deep breath, smelling the air. Both of their eyes flashed with desire. "May I help you, my queen?" Henry blurted. Asher looked at me knowingly and Henry cleared his throat, being brought back to the world around him.

"Give me ten minutes and we'll be down. Lunch is ready and is on the table." I smiled and quickly went up the stairs, stopping at the top when I saw a third body enter through the door.

"Finally," Drake grumbled, pushing past us to the food. I sadly watched as he went to the dining room, out of sight, before walking into my room with Lany behind me.

"He'll be okay." I nod, knowing he will, but I couldn't get the feeling he won't out of my head. "Let's get you cleaned up and fed." He took my hand and led me into my bathroom, slowly undressing me, kissing my back, and pulling my shirt up. I turned to press him against the closed door, and I un-buttoned his shirt, sliding off him.

"Excuse me, ma'am. It seems you're missing something." He smirked down at me as he pulled my thong out from his back pocket. I giggle and shake my head as I undo his pants.

"Are you needing them? I see you're not wearing any-thing under your jeans." I teased, and he put his hand on his chin in contemplation.

108

"I think I'd stretch them out too much." He dropped them, and I pulled his pants down, going to my knees in front of him. "Well, isn't this a familiar sight?" His hands went to my hair. Standing up, I shimmy out of my skirt, so I was naked in front of the similarly nude male. His eyes raked me up and down, and his hand went to the scar on my abdomen. "I hope you'll be able to talk about what happened while you were away one day." He kissed me softly and walked me back into the shower. I took a breath and turned on the water so it waterfalled on us. One day I will tell him. One day all of the Windsors will know. I welcomed the distraction when he got to his knees in front of me, grabbing my loofah and body wash. "Let me get you cleaned down here."

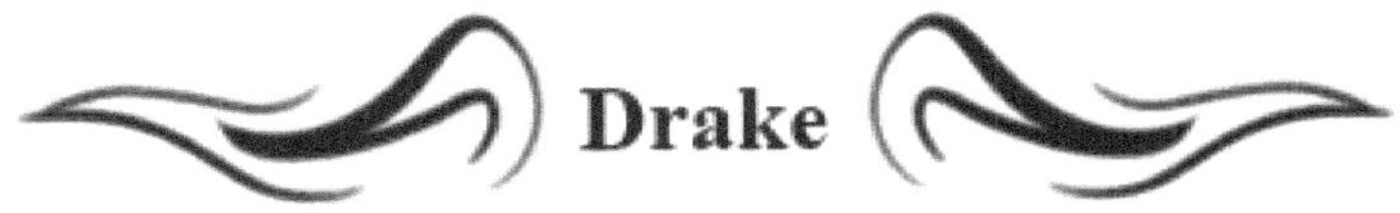

Drake

It only took a few minutes for Drake to lose his appetite; his hands on his knees, squeezing tightly as he heard the moans from upstairs. Those moans sounded familiar yet foreign, as if he heard double speaking. Everything in his mind contradicted, causing his temple to pound. Looking at his half-eaten plate of spaghetti, Drake decided he was done eating, his stomach agreeing with his headache. Slamming his hands on the table as he stood caused Henry and Asher to look up at him, stopping their conversation. Ignoring the looks and silent questions directed at him, he chose to storm out the back door, slamming it behind him. Drake didn't leave the property as instructed, but that didn't mean he couldn't walk around outside to try to clear his mind again. The anger in his chest was a fire he couldn't smother; a growing heat almost overwhelmed him as he sat on a bench in the garden.

Amelia

Putting my wet hair up in a messy bun, Lany walked up behind me, sliding his hands onto my hips and kissing my neck. "You are beautiful, Lia." I lock eyes with him in the mirror and smile, rolling my eyes.

"We need to eat."

"I've already eaten, but I could eat some more." He nuzzled his face into my shoulder, making me think about how I was leaning against the shower wall as he ate me out not five minutes ago.

"Later." I turn around in his grasp to kiss him.

"We'll see." The redhead stepped back, smirking, and went into my room. I followed, going to my closet while he grabbed a pair of basketball shorts from the one drawer in my dresser filled with the boys' clothes I've stolen through the years.

"You're not leaving again, are you?" He asked, and we both looked at my suitcase and backpack in my practically empty closet.

"No. They can't make me leave again." These past few days have cemented that fact in my brain. I'd rather fight and claw my way out than let some mages threaten my life again.

He nods but doesn't say anything. I know they all worry about me disappearing again, but I won't let that happen. We are in this for the long haul. Lany followed me back down the stairs to where the others were eating, seeing Drake had already left the table.

"Nice of you to finally join us." Asher smiled at me, chuckling.

"The food was getting cold. Don't want your hard work, slaving over the stove, to go to waste." Henry reached out and brought my hand up to his lips, kissing my knuckles, and winked up at me.

Looking over at the third place set with food still on it, sorrow filled my lungs, making it harder to breathe. "I guess he wasn't that hungry." Grabbing an empty plate, I serve myself and sit at the head of the table. Halfway through eating, my phone lit up, buzzing on the table with Uncle Nick's picture flashing twice on the screen.

Uncle: *Doc just called. Said his last patient didn't need as much as he thought. Should be there by early afternoon tomorrow.*

Looking up, I smiled as hope coursed through my nerves and I relayed the good news.

"Someone should go tell Drake," Henry chimed, causing three sets of eyes to fall on me.

"Me? He doesn't even want to be in the same room as me, let alone talk to me."

"You're the one who should do it." Asher put his hand on mine. "You never know, he might surprise you."

Sighing, I stood and pointed to my half-eaten plate of food. "Then one of you will deal with this while I go and deal with that."

Henry stood quickly. "I'll take care of it."

"I'll help you," Asher piped up, picking up the plate.

Nodding, I walked through the small reading area with a fireplace to the back door and took a deep breath of the fresh outside air. It was still nice out, a slight breeze keeping it cool. I could see the blonde, shoulder-length hair slowly moving through the garden entrance. "Drake!" I called out, causing him to stop moving and look back at me. As I jogged to get closer, I could see the glossiness of his eyes fade slightly.

Drake smiled and began to open his arms, but stopped, hesitantly. "Amelia?" His voice was doubtful.

Pausing, I blinked. "You, you recognize me?"

"I don't know. You look and sound like you. How do I know it's you, though?" He crossed his arms. His body language screamed defensive but with authority. Despite his fear, he was still the one in charge.

I had to take a deep breath to calm my nerves. What if this was just like when I cried in his arms at the lake before the mage showed up? "You're within the boundaries of our land. Her magic won't work here." I repeated the words my uncle had to repeat to me to help calm my nerves over the past few days.

"And what if you're just someone else, trying to convince me? How can I tell that this," He gestured around him, "isn't just some spell in my head like y'all are convincing me happened with," He paused, and I could tell he was doing his best to search his foggy memory. "Lindsay?" Drake's voice was filled with pent-up emotion that came out as aggression and slight fear, though I wouldn't ever tell him that.

I knew this wasn't going to be easy, but the tearing feeling in my chest wasn't what I expected. "I... I just wanted to tell you the doctor will be here tomorrow. Uncle Nick says early afternoon." I didn't like how my voice cracked as I spoke. This was why I didn't want to be the one telling him. It hurt too much. I took a moment to look into his eyes and could tell so much was going through his mind. Too many doubts. I couldn't cry in front of him, not when he was fighting himself mentally as to what was and wasn't real. Turning and running back to the backdoor, I wished he'd run after me, but he wasn't my Drake yet, and until he was back to himself, I didn't want him to feel forced into anything.

The night came fast, and I found myself in bed, head on Henry's lap, with him petting my hair softly. The movie on the television was lulling me to sleep, but the voices from downstairs kept me awake as I tried to listen in. The frustration in Drake's voice was evident as he tried to keep calm. I was thrilled the doctor was coming tomorrow, but I couldn't help but think about how Drake would cope after the doctor helped him. I gently squeezed Henry's thigh, causing him to look down at me. "What's up?"

"Drake said something that keeps bothering me," I whispered. "How do we prove that what he's experiencing now isn't some mind magic? The very same he's been experiencing for the past two years?"

"I'm sure the doctor will help with that when he gets here. Don't take anything Drake says right now too seriously. He's under a lot of pressure and isn't allowed to let any of it out. You've been able to through sex instead of shifting. He's had no way of letting go of any pent-up frustration or energy." I nodded, hoping the night would pass by quickly for all of us.

Sunday, October 8th, 2017

In the morning, I was awoken by the smell of breakfast cooking downstairs. Keeping my eyes closed, I reveled in the warmth that the two cuddled up against me exuded. Henry was on his back, and I was curled up against him with Asher's arm wrapped around my waist and his chest pressed against my back. Unfortunately, my bladder yelled louder for atten-tion, making my decision for me to get out of bed. Groaning softly, I slowly tried to weasel my way out from between them, so I didn't wake either of them.

"Good morning, Darlin'." Asher yawned and stretched, making me curse myself inwardly for waking him. The red-head rolled over to the edge of the bed before getting up. "Sleep well?" He walked over and gave me a quick kiss.

"I always have amazing sleep with you guys around." The past week had been the best sleep I'd had in years. I smiled up at him and headed to the bathroom while Asher headed downstairs. When I left the bathroom, Henry was still passed out, now sprawled across the large bed. He unconsciously found one of the body pillows in his sleep and had pulled it on top of himself, cuddling it close to him. It made me smile at how adorable he could be. Letting the man sleep, I went downstairs to see Uncle Nick still home and cooking French toast. Drake was also still passed out on the couch in the living room, making me wonder what time it was.

"Good morning," Uncle Nick chimed, back turned as he pulled out different containers of fresh fruit.

I carefully tiptoed from the stairs into the kitchen, not wanting to wake another Windsor male. "Morning. What time is it?" Rubbing the sleep from my eyes, I looked outside to see it was light out, so it couldn't be too early in the morning.

"It's only…" Uncle Nick glanced at his watch. "Seven forty-three."

"Why is Drake still asleep, and why are you home?" I tiredly plopped into one of the seats at the small breakfast table next to Asher.

"I'm allowed to have a day off every now and then." Nick chuckled. "As for him," He gestured with his elbow towards the alpha. "He was up late last night. I gave him some meds to help his headache and to help him sleep."

"Hopefully it's a good sign?" My hopefulness didn't reach my eyes as I looked at the back of the couch Drake was sleeping on.

"Hopefully. Logan, the doctor, is driving down from Indiana today. He'll be here just after noon." He placed the plate piled high with French toast on the table along with three empty plates. We ate breakfast quietly, each silently praying for the morning to pass by fast.

When done, Asher left to check in with his mother at the visitor center and afterward help Lany with the rounds, while Nick went back to cooking, knowing that the two sleeping shifters would be hungry when they woke up. "After I'm done with these, I'm going to do some paperwork to get our own vehicle again." He looked at me, and I looked at the rental still in the driveway. For a moment, I wondered what happened to the vehicle we abandoned at the airport two years ago, but I didn't really want to know if I was honest. It didn't matter.

I, once again, quietly snuck up the stairs, thankful that none of them creaked when walked on. Thank God for the magic preserving the wood of the cabin. Henry was still sleeping when I walked into my room, but had discarded the body pillow and had his arms above his head. I could see the morning wood he had and inwardly moaned. Closing the door with a silent click, I walked over to the foot of the bed and crawled on top of him, placing my hands to keep his wrists above his head when he woke. He jolted awake at the feeling of being restrained, but immediately relaxed when he saw it was me. "Good morning, sleeping beauty." I kissed his neck, moving my hips to grind on him, a thin blanket and my shorts separating us since he hated sleeping with clothes on.

"You're awake early." His voice was groggy, filled with sleep. "To what do I owe this pleasure?" He looked up at my hands holding his wrists and grinned before looking back up at me.

"First, you tell me about the dream you were having." I kissed and nipped his neck playfully.

He let out a soft moan. "It was about you." His breath hitched as I bit his neck, causing a jolt of pleasure to go down my spine.

"Continue." I purred, moving his hands together so I could hold them with one hand. My other hand went to his hair to run my fingers through it.

I watched as Henry found it harder to speak coherently the more I rediscovered his pleasure spots, moving my hand down and lightly grazing one of his nipples. "You had tied me to... the bed and… oh, fuck, Ma'am."

"Yes?" I had my hand wrapped around his cock now, my thumb grazing the tip.

"Please," His hips bucked. "My Queen, use me."

"You still haven't told me about your dream." I got off of him and turned my back to him, causing Henry to whimper.

"You sat on my face and made me eat you out, teasing me." I could hear the panting in his breaths as he spoke. Taking a quick glance behind me, I could see he hadn't moved.

"Such a good boy. Is that what you want?" I turned around, now only in my black, sheer, lace bra and matching thong. "Do you want to eat me out?"

"I want you to cum on my face." Henry got up, getting to all fours and crawling to the edge of the bed. "I want you to ride me, using me for your pleasure."

"You wanna be my good boy?" I put my hand on his cheek and tapped a couple of times.

"Yes, my Queen." His southern drawl became more prominent as he spoke.

Grinning, I pushed him back, causing him to lie back down. "Such an obedient little toy, aren't you?" Henry nodded, watching me. I slowly took off my pair of shorts "Is this what you want?" I straddled him, my wet folds teasing the length of his cock as I slowly moved my hips, making his cock slick with my arousal. "Or would you rather eat me out?" Seeing him do his best to concentrate on my words rather than actions sent me thrills. The empowering feeling of being in control of something, being able to turn this big, strong man into a whimpering pile of mush, was exhilarating.

"Please," he started to beg, "I want to please you. I want to make you cum over and over." Henry looked up at me, pleadingly. "I want you to use my mouth and sit on my face."

"Since you've been such a good boy, I'll grant you your request." I moved up, straddling his face, moaning when he licked me. My hands went to his hair as he sucked and licked my clit. "Fuck yes. You taste so good." The moans he was making only heightened my pleasure.

Henry darted his tongue out, past my folds, and tongue fucked me, switching between that and lightly nipping at my clit. Not too much pressure, but just enough to get a gasp and

118

small yelp from my lips. Oh, fuck I was close. He moved his hands to massage my legs and pressed me further against his mouth, so I was fully riding his face.

He moaned, and it sent just enough of a vibration to put me over the edge. I moved my hips, riding out my orgasm, and he licked up as much of my juices as he could. I move off of him and smile, his cheeks glistening with my juices. Leaning down, I licked his cheek and kissed him, moaning as he deepened the kiss. My hand trailed down his chest to his nipple and pinched, smirking when he gasped and arched his back. "You like that?" I tease, locking eyes with him.

"Yes," He breathed out.

"Do you want more?"

"Please." He arched his back more as I squeezed the other nipple. "Fuck. Yes." Henry moaned. I absolutely loved the noises I could get from this man.

"Tell me." I rub around his nipples as I move to straddle him. Grinding against his cock, I let out a moan.

"My Queen." He groaned, closing his eyes.

I tisk, removing my hands from his chest and stopping my movement against him. "Keep those pretty blue eyes open for me." Out of the fear of them, Henry's eyes hardest to turn to slits, seemingly unaffected by hoe turned on he was, making it all the more pleasurable when they did.

He looked up at me, following my order. "Yes, Ma'am." Henry's whimper as his hips tried to move for friction made me smirk, and I lifted my hips so he wouldn't get it. "Please." His eyes pleaded for more. At the sound of a car in the driveway, I peeked out the window to see my uncle leaving and smiled down at the whimpering male beneath me, knowing we didn't need to be quiet.

"Please, what?"

"Please! I need to be inside you. I need to feel your pussy around my cock."

Leaning down, I kiss his neck, just under his ear, and whisper, "You're not allowed to cum until I say you can."

His eyes widened, and I slipped him inside of me, gasping at the feeling. He was slightly thicker than his brothers, definitely thicker than the small vibrator I've had over the past two years, and damn did it feel amazing. "Henry!" I slowly moved against him and saw how his fists clenched in the sheets as he tried not to move. "Such a good fuck toy." I moan. "Put your hands above your head."

Henry looked up at me, slowly moving his arms up and gripping the edge of the bed above his head. His blue eyes pleading, begging for more. "My Queen." He breathed out. "Please." Henry arched his back as I started bouncing on his cock. "Yes." He hissed, and I wasn't going to hold back anymore. I pinched his nipples as I rocked and bounced, using his body to give me pleasure.

"Such a good…mmm, good fuck toy." I could feel another orgasm and I leaned down and bit his peck, moaning and sucking to mark him.

"Ahh." He groaned and arched into me. "Amelia." His breathing was quick, and I could tell he was as close as I was.

"Do you want to cum?"

120

"I'm so close." He whimpered, unable to control the bucking of his hips.

"Not yet, toy." I lick where I bit, seeing the red curves of my teeth marks. "I need to cum first."

"Always." He breathed out, and I could see the veins in his arms bulging with how tightly he was gripping the bed to hold back.

"So, good." I moan. "Watch me cum on your dick." I lean back as I keep moving up and down. My hand reaches down to my clit and starts rubbing while my other hand went to one of my breasts, squeezing before giving the other the same treatment. I watched as the blonde struggled to keep his eyes open, lost in ecstasy. It was when he opened his yes and I saw his beautiful red slits that I lost control. Cumming hard, I cry out and buck on his cock. His groans push me off the edge, and I ride out another orgasm. Before I allowed myself to collapse onto him, I got off and licked his cock from base to tip. "Cum in my mouth." I suck his tip and with only two pumps of my hand, cum filled my mouth and I proudly swallowed it.

I crawled up next to him and he put his arm around me, both of us breathless. Looking up at him, I smiled, and he leaned down to kiss me, tasting the mix of our cum just as I did.

"Fuck that felt exhilarating," I whispered in his ear.

Henry chuckled, "Would you like me to help clean you?"

I nodded, slowly closing my eyes. He slowly moved, carrying

me to the bathroom and placing me on the cool countertop before taking a cloth and cleaning me up.

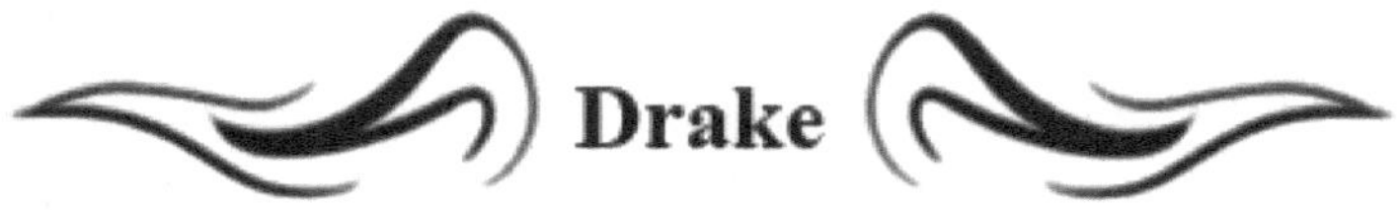

Drake

Downstairs, Drake groaned. His head hurt more than it did last night, and the sounds he woke up to caused him to get hot and bothered. All of his brothers have had her multiple times now. They hadn't been with anyone since Amelia first left. Was this woman actually who she said she is? He growled as he stumbled to the bathroom down the hall and didn't bother to turn the light on. Leaning against the cool, tile wall, thankful for the temperature difference, Drake took a deep breath. It was also silent in this room, allowing him to ignore the activities he knew were above him. After several more deep breaths, he sat on the floor, his head in his hands. The darkness of the bathroom surrounding him didn't compare to the darkness he felt as his body went limp.

Chapter Seven

HENRY FOLLOWED ME DOWN THE STAIRS AND into the kitchen. "That's weird," I picked up Nick's phone on the counter. "He left without his phone." I shrugged, turning to Henry as he got the leftovers Nick made, out of the fridge. "And Drake didn't eat." Had Drake left with Uncle Nick? No, Drake wasn't allowed to leave the property, Uncle Nick wouldn't have brought him with, but the alpha wasn't lying on the couch anymore either. My brain racked through if I'd heard him leave the house or not and a pit of nerves formed in my stomach. I looked around, quickly running out of the front door, yelling for Drake. I didn't leave the front porch as I cupped my hands around my mouth to call out to Drake again. If he was here, he'd hear me. Henry put a hand on my shoulder, looking at me with worry. "I don't have a good feeling." With the look growing with concern, I explained quickly. "He's missing and didn't eat."

"Let's not worry before we have to. He could just have needed some air before he wanted to eat, or he could just be in the restroom. Henry's soothing words helped, but I knew something was wrong. Panic had me feeling the fast pounding of my heart in my chest. I kept good track of the alpha's whereabouts these past few days, this being the only time I didn't know where he was.

I looked out and still didn't see the alpha walking in the front yard, so I decided to check the bathroom before going to the backyard. Rushing to the hall restroom, I found the doorknob was locked. Knocking, I called out, "Drake? Drake, are you in there?" The wavering of my voice made me inwardly curse at how close to tears I was. After there was no answer, I pounded on the door. "Drake!" Henry rushed over and pulled out a knife, using it to slip the door open. I pushed him out of the way once he was done and turned on the light to see Drake lying, passed out, on the ground. "Shit, shit, shit!" I got down and checked his pulse, watching his chest. Seeing he was still breathing and that it was a regular breath, I looked up at Henry, who had already gotten down to pick up his brother. I followed the tall male, cursing Lindsay under my breath. I didn't know how, but she is the one who caused this. If she could cause this while he was here, what else could she do? Were the wards not enough against her magic? Did she have that much of a hold on the alpha's mind?

"Amelia, get a rag damp, he feels warm." Henry put his brother down on the pull-out and took off the shirt his brother was wearing. I did just that and, after giving the rag to Henry, started pacing with my mind racing about what could have caused this. And why hadn't Uncle Nick taken his damned phone with him?

Speak of the Devil and he shall appear. The sound of Uncle Nick pulling up in the driveway had me sprinting out the front door. I practically pulled the door off the hinges when he parked. "Drake won't wake up!" I yelled, and Uncle Nick quickly unclicked his seatbelt. I dragged him inside, to the living room.

"I'll call Logan. He's still probably a few hours out, though. He went to the kitchen, where his phone was forgotten on the counter.

"Why the Fuck didn't you have your phone?!" I yelled, letting my emotions take control.

"I didn't mean to forget it. I came back once I realized I didn't have it." I needed to punch something, anything, but I knew that wouldn't bring me the relief I was looking for. No, I needed to go and find that God damned mage and kill her. "I'll hunt their entire family down," I growled, causing Henry to stand and get between me and the door.

"I won't let you do that."

"Not you too?!" I had tears burning my eyes, threatening to fall. How dare anyone, let alone one of my boys get in my way of killing the cunt who caused us all of this pain. "Do you not think we'd just be better if she and her coven were dead?"

"Not yet. I want to make her suffer too, and she'll get her dues, but now is not the time. Right now, we need to inform Mom, Asher, and Landon. I'll go get Mom, and you go and get the other two. Drake is in good hands with your uncle."

He was right, and we both knew it. Shifting would help me calm down, and those three needed to know what was happening with the eldest Windsor boy. "Okay." I sighed and gave Drake a last glance before walking out the door.

I'll admit, I was tempted to go find the mage instead of Lany and Asher, but the boys needed me, and they took priority. Shifting, I flew just above the trees. "Landon!" I mentally called out. "Asher!" One of them should be close enough to hear me, but with every passing second and still no answer, I started to panic. Had she gotten to them, too? Was that why she'd taken this chance to attack Drake? "Emergency!" My mental cry sounded more like a sob as I flew North, past the Kentucky line. Trying to push my thoughts further, as if that would help, I called out for the both of them again. "Help!"

"What's wrong?" Asher's words flooded my mind, and I almost dropped out of the sky due to the relief I felt.

"Drake! Something is wrong with Drake." A golden dragon flew up next to me, and soon followed a red one.

"What's wrong with Drake?" Landon asked as they followed me back towards the cabin.

"Henry and I found him unconscious in a dark bathroom. He won't wake up. He's overheating." Tears started to

126

form again in my eyes, but I did my best to blink them away. When we landed, I watched as a golden and a red dragon landed on the other side of the property. All of us shifted back into our human forms and went to the barrel of clothes. Mable slipped on a dress while the rest of us quickly put on a pair of shorts. Grabbing the drawstrings, I tightened the oversized pair I wore around me.

Nick had adjusted Drake on the pullout couch, making it look like a makeshift hospital bed. He attached a thermometer to Drake's head and a pulse oximeter on his finger. Ice packs and wet towels were on Drake's forehead and chest, and wet spots grew around the alpha's unconscious body. Taking a few seconds, I watched the subtle rise and fall of his chest, thankful he was still alive. "Logan is about two hours away now and said he has the necessary equipment to help. He says it's a mixture of the lingering effect of Lindsay's magic, along with his body building up too much druidic magic. It's why he's burning up; the dragon wants to come out, but he's fighting the shift."

Henry quickly went to the closet and pulled out a light blanket, went to the bathroom to make it damp with cool water, and brought it back to put on his older brother. I started pacing again. Shifting had helped relieve the aggression, but I could still feel the energy radiating off me. Glancing at Drake each time I turned in my pacing, I made sure his chest still showed his breathing. If my alpha dies today, so does she.

The two hours passed by too slowly as we changed out the ice packs, Drake's heat melting them faster than they could freeze, and getting worse as time passed. I had lashed out at everyone after the first hour, storming out and deciding to pace the entire border of the property like a caged animal. Not for the first time, I looked in the direction of town, where I knew that absolute cunt lived. I could easily fly to town and kill the mage who did this. What stopped me was knowing at least one of my boys kept an eye on me as I walked the border of the property. They would stop me if I went too far.

When the SUV drove up, I ran to the front porch, hope filling my chest. It took everything inside me not to bite the head off of the man for taking so long, but I knew, deep down, he had arrived as quickly as he could. Right now, I didn't listen to that voice. I would simply chew him out after he helped Drake. "All hands on deck!" I yelled at the window and ran back to the dark blue F.E. Ophiotaurus. The dark blue SUV backed up to the front porch, and as soon as it stopped, the tailgate lifted, revealing several black boxes with yellow lids. A tall man with short blonde hair slicked back and deep blue eyes hidden behind a pair of thick-framed glasses got out of the vehicle.

"Help with the boxes in the trunk. I'll grab immediate necessities from the back seat." His deep voice surprised me, but I did as I was told, repeating the instructions to the boys when they arrived next to me. The Doc grabbed his bag and a small medical box before heading inside. I was quick to follow him in, carrying one of the larger boxes. Mable replaced a warmed ice pack with a cooler one while Uncle Nick rubbed her back reassuringly. "Doctor Logan Chester-Cooper at your service, Ma'am." He tipped his head in her direction. "Let's get the boy hooked up to stabilize his body before I work on his mind." He waved his hand over the medical box, and it transformed into a vitals monitor, the appropriate utensils becoming available.

Uncle Nick watched, brows scrunched in confusion. "How did that work? Magic like that shouldn't be able to work on this property."

Logan smirked. "Not magic. Angel technology is far more useful than what is common around these parts." He rolled the machine closer to the bed and started hooking it up to Drake. He quickly took notes on the monitor and nodded, more to himself since he didn't say anything. "How long has he not been shifting, did you say?"

"Four days." I chimed in, having put a second box down. He nodded and kept making notes. "Will you be able to help him?"

"You're lucky that, where I'm from, they have special medications for dragons in similar cases." He pointed to one of the boxes labeled *Mystic Cooling.* "In that box, I have pouches of solutions. Could you bring me two of the ones that say Gold?"

"He's also half red if that means anything," Mable spoke up.

Nodding, the doctor corrected himself. "Two gold and one red."

Happy to feel as if anything I am doing is helping, I quickly grab the bags of clear liquid. "What will these do?" I watched as he hooked up each bag to the monitor.

"Could you tie this around his upper arm?" Doctor Logan handed what looked like a thick rubber band to my uncle. "These will help cool his body temperature by relieving the pent-up druidic magic." I watched as he expertly inserted a cannula into Drake's hand and hooked up one of the pouches labeled red. I look at the three pouches, still not completely understanding. "Shifting usually releases the excess energy, but when a shifter doesn't shift, it builds up, and," He looked down at the unconscious man, "in fire-attuned dragons, they overheat." Fire attuned? It made me wonder what would happen to me. I also hadn't shifted in a couple of days, but didn't feel off or anything.

Sighing, I look at my uncle, wondering why we didn't know this. He was a doctor, wasn't he? He was adept with druidic magic for fuck's sake. There wasn't any mention of this happening while we were at my grandfather's property either.

"I'm sorry, Amelia." Uncle Nick walked over and guided me to the recliner where Asher was sitting, and I sat on the armrest, unable to look away from Drake. Asher rubbed my back reassuringly. "I didn't know. I've never heard of such things happening…" Uncle Nick looked at me regretfully. I know it wasn't his fault. "I've always been in places that anyone could shift if they needed to."

"That doesn't surprise me," Doctor Chester remarked, not bothering to look up from the monitor he was taking notes on. "Shifters like you are comparatively new as a species."

"What do you mean by that?" Mable questioned. I looked him over, and, although he seemed to hear her, didn't answer. How complicated was it? How much more about us did he know that we didn't?

Finished with the monitor, Logan looked around at where the different boxes were put before walking to a box, pulling out a film with black dots, and started to unstick them from the film to stick them onto Drake's forehead. "I can explain further, but trying to undo the spells the mage has cast on him will take a long time." When he was done putting them on Drake's forehead, Doctor Logan started placing them onto his own forehead, mimicking the placement of Drake's. "I will need to not be disturbed while doing this." He put on a pair of cloth gloves and sat on the back of the couch, above where Drake lay. Logan closed his eyes, concentrating when blue streaks of lightning connected from his fingertips, through the gloves, to the dots on Drake's head.

Uncle Nick left the room, pulling his phone out before closing the front door behind him. Mable sat on the loveseat, watching, looking hopeless. Watching her broke my heart, knowing the feeling of being a helpless mother. Asher squeezed my hand, and I smiled at him, tears forming in my eyes. I had to tell them. They deserved to know. Was right now the best time, though? Have them learn about what could have been while they are worrying about the here and now? "Come on," Asher whispered in my ear, but when I didn't move, he picked me up and carried me up the stairs, Henry and Landon following us to my room.

With my head resting in Asher's lap, his hands nervously running through my hair to soothe not only me but himself as well. Landon's head was on my lap, holding my hand and squeezing it every so often. Henry was sitting criss-cross at my feet, rubbing them. The room was suffocating with worry. Hours passed like days as we all waited. Uncle Nick had popped in periodically to check on us while Henry went to check on Mable every thirty minutes or so.

Uncle Nick knocked on the door while slowly opening it. I was still on the bed, but now I was curled up against Lany's lap, and Asher had taken to folding the clothes in the donation pile we still hadn't taken out yet. "Doc says Drake should be waking up soon." I couldn't get out of bed fast enough, pushing Uncle Nick out of the way with Lany and Nick on my heels.

Drake slowly sat up with the help of Logan and rubbed his head. I paused at the bottom of the stairs, watching, but the two Windsor boys behind me brushed passed me to be next to their brother. "Just take it slow." Logan coached, taking the dots from Drake's forehead.

"What the fuck happened?" He growled, looking around. "Why am I here?"

"Your mind should catch up to you soon, but to shorten it up, you've been under a few spells altering your memory for about two years. With the help of angelic technology and dra-conic medicine, you should have a speedy recovery. To be honest, I give it a few hours until your mind catches up with you. When it does, I recommend you go out and shift for a few hours. Your brothers can accompany you, and so can Amelia if you wish. You won't be fully healed mentally or physically for a few days, but the worst of it should be over and done with after the first few hours. In the meantime, take it easy. I'm staying in town at the Owl's Inn if you need me. I'll leave the boxes here, however, in case they are needed."

"Amelia?" Drake looked around quickly but grabbed his head, groaning. "Fuck this room's spinning."

"I'm here." I ran up to him, hope bubbling inside of me that he'd see me for me. All doubt in my mind about what his reaction would be dissipated when his eyes locked onto mine. His smile was so genuine that it brought tears to my eyes. "And you are too." He opened his arms, and I melted into him, relishing the feeling of being surrounded by him. The others walked into the dining room to speak, but I couldn't care less right now. Drake was here, both physically and mentally, and that's all that mattered right now.

"You're alive," Drake whispered into my hair, making me wonder what all was going through his mind, the torment he'd put himself through. I figure, though, it would be best to start at the beginning.

"I'm sorry. It wasn't you. I couldn't reach out to you. I wanted to, begged to. There's so much to tell you."

"Shh." He pet my hair. "You're okay. You're safe." Drake's soft words were laced with his alpha presence, helping soothe me, making me wonder if it helped him too.

After a few minutes, everyone came back in with Logan speaking, "Yes. Now, I haven't eaten since yesterday, and I've driven nonstop in my hurry to get here. I'm going to go to the inn, eat, and pass out if you don't mind. If something changes for the worse, you can call me. Otherwise, we can continue this talk tomorrow." He grabbed his bag and nodded towards Drake. "Remember, in a few hours, you'll feel a lot of energy that will need to be let out. I recommend shifting. Nick has a ring to give you that blocks the mage's magic for the next few days. If you have any issues, call me, and I'll be here in 10 minutes.

"Thank you, Doc." Drake nodded back. He looked back down at me, and I could see in his eyes that he was tired. "I think I need a nap. You promise to be here when I wake up?"

"I promise." I smile. "I might be in the kitchen or in my room, though, but you get some rest and we can shift when you wake up." I looked up and could feel the relief radiating off the others when Drake laid down.

"Well, I do believe he's in good hands now." Henry smiled at me, and I stood from the pull-out. "We need to go do our rounds. Make sure all the trails are clear."

"I know. I'll keep an eye on him and will let y'all know if anything happens. Stay safe." With a kiss goodbye to each of them, they went to do their rounds, having been interrupted earlier.

"It's been a long day." Mable hugged me tightly. "I'm going to go to bed, now that I can sleep easy, knowing he's going to be okay."

"Yeah." I choke on my words. "He'll be okay."

"I have an early shift in the morning, so I'll also be hitting the hay." Uncle Nick gave me a quick hug and a kiss on the forehead. "You get some sleep too, okay?"

"Thank you, I'll try." I watched them both head into Uncle Nick's room. Looking back down at the sleeping Windsor, I felt the effect of the day hit me. All of the stress had finally caught up to me. Drudging up the stairs, I went to my room and sleep fell upon me as quickly as I fell upon the bed.

The slamming of my bedroom door woke me up, the raging alpha pacing at the front of my bed. Sitting up, I rubbed the sleep from my eyes. "Good morning, Sunshine," I murmured, still processing what was happening. "You're awake." In my half-asleep state, I noticed it was still dark out.

"It's true, isn't it? All of it? You didn't come back a couple of months after disappearing? I was enchanted?" His volume rose with every question. I could tell he had too much energy in him and remembered what the doctor said about him needing to shift. Frowning as his questions continued, I listened to how his rambling questions transitioned from anger at Lindsay to anger towards himself, implying that he was incompetent. I knew he was confused, and the confusion in his mind bothered him, but the way he spoke about himself wasn't going to fly. No one was going to talk about my boys that way. "Shut up! Drake, it's okay. You didn't know better, but now you do. It wasn't your fault. None of it was your fault. Stop blaming yourself! You're still healing. Doctor Chester said it would take a couple more days. We'll go shift, and you'll be able to clear your mind."

Oh, was I wrong in my assumption of his need to shift. Drake stopped and turned to me. "Quiet." He commanded, his voice oozing with authority, but also lost the anger he had when he was speaking about himself. Drake was never someone to direct anger towards something that wasn't the cause. "That… that witch. I should have realized. I should have known." He growled. "You don't understand. I haven't been able to *spread my wings with her*." He closed his eyes, looked up, and took another deep breath, letting out a low growl. "How could I be such a fucking idiot?" He cursed himself. Red and golden scales faded in and out along his forearms as he clenched his fists.

"Don't talk about yourself that way! You're a smart man." I stood, getting in front of him, tired of hearing him degrade himself. This wasn't like him; Drake had always been arrogant. I took a step closer to the man to try to help calm him. "We can work through this." Being this close, I could see how tense he was.

With a swift movement, my back was pressed firmly against the wall, wrists being held above my head by one of his hands. My breath hitched with Drake's mouth hovering over the crook of my neck. "I don't think you heard me right." His voice, low and husky in my ear. Placing a knee between mine to spread my legs slightly, he brought his knee up,

136

rubbing against my crotch. Holy fuck, the heat in his eyes traveled down to my core as I felt myself get wet for this man. "She's not…" He leaned further in and took a deep breath, breathing in my scent. Speaking even softer next to my ear, he growled, "As much of a good girl, like you are." Fuck, how those words flipped a light switch inside of me and I arched my back, silently pleading for his touch. Biting my lip, I whimpered with need. His hand cupping my cheek had me opening my eyes. "Does my baby need something?"

"Please." I breathed out, knowing he could hear me. The feeling of his leg against my pussy was all I could get as he held still. I started to move my hips, needing any semblance of pleasure.

"Ahh, ahh, ahh." He tisked and moved his leg mere inches away from where I needed it, but still pinned me to the wall. "It seems you've forgotten how to ask for something." Letting go of my wrists, Drake took a step back. I didn't dare move as he looked me up and down. "We can't forget our manners, can we?" I suddenly wish I slept naked. Naked was natural, I didn't care if I walked around naked, but sleeping? Give me a cozy oversized T-shirt, please. Tonight, I was wearing one of Lany's old cotton shirts, the kind that only got softer with age, making me feel vulnerable against Drake's gaze. His arms crossed over his chest, bringing my attention back to him. One of his eyebrows was raised, as if asking what was going through my mind.

"Please, I need you." I locked eyes with him, his eyes flickering between his typical golden orbs and shining golden slits. He needed me more than I needed him, and he was still fighting some war in his mind. "Master, I need you to fuck me." He needed to fuck me.

"Oh really?" The alpha smirked, giving me another once-over. "When was the last time you came?"

Blushing, I recalled this morning, oh, how long ago it felt. Taking control with Henry when I felt like I had no power at all. "This morning."

He chuckled before leaning into me again, his breath sending shivers down my spine. "You're such a needy little thing, aren't you?" Drake whispered, causing a whimper to escape from me.

"Yes." I leaned into him, my knees going weak.

"Yes, what?" I could feel him smirk against me, trailing kisses down my neck.

"I'm so fucking needy."

"Since you don't *need* me to cum," He backed away and pointed to the bed. "Strip. Make yourself cum for me." There was a venom in his voice I'd never heard before, but looking him up and down, I could see how hard he was by the bulge in his pants. I practically tore my clothes off as I got into bed, feeling a spark in the air I hadn't felt before as his eyes narrowed at my naked form, examining every inch of my skin. I could tell when he registered my scar.

"Drake." I moaned to distract him and brought my hand down to my wet folds.

"Fuck." He groaned and his hands gripped the end of my bed, his knuckles turning white. I spread wide for him and

138

slipped a finger inside myself, arching my back in exaggeration. I didn't want my finger; I wanted his cock.

"Add another," Drake demanded lowly, a growl escaping from his chest. Adding another finger inside me, I started moving. It felt good, don't get me wrong, but it was the anticipation of more that really kept me going. I didn't dare look away as I used my thumb to rub my sensitive nub, moaning out his name. "Tell me what you need, Baby."

"You. Please, I need your cock inside of me." Panting, I could feel the pressure in me building.

"Good girl." He smirked, slowly pulling down his sweatpants, revealing his hard cock for me. I rubbed my pussy faster, I watching his hand wrap around his length, slowly moving up and down. "Keep it up and you'll get a reward."

I moaned, inching closer to the edge. "Master, may I cum?" My eyes didn't leave his cock as precum leaked from the tip.

"Yes." He growled, and I went over the edge, my back arching and eyes closing for the first time. It was the first time I'd gotten myself off since I'd come back.

"Such a good girl for me." He chuckled, and I looked up at him in a daze. "Come here." Letting go of his cock, Drake motioned with one finger, and I crawled over to the edge of the bed, where he gripped the bed frame. "How did that feel?"

"It felt good." I couldn't help but whimper. I watched as golden and red scales faded in and out across his arms and chest when he breathed on his arms and chest. It brought back the thought of him needing to shift. "Drake," I say, concerned. His eyes were shifted and though he seemed in control of himself, he looked almost crazed.

"Baby, I need you to be quiet." He leaned down and kissed me, a hand going to the back of my head to grip my hair. "You are going to take this dick like the good girl you are." A soft moan escaped my lips. "Did you want to suck it first, or are you wet enough for me already?" Looking with pleading eyes, I look between his eyes and cock.

"Take me." Within a blink of an eye, I was flipped onto my stomach with my ass raised, and Drake kneeled on the bed behind me.

He gave my ass a spank before gripping my hips. His fingers shifted to claws, digging into my hips. "Mine." He growled before shoving his cock in my pussy, filling me. The grip on me was sure to leave a few bruises, but they would heal after we shifted. My moans got louder as he went faster. "Fuck, Baby, that's it. Take it all." I could feel the bed sheets underneath me, rubbing against my hardened nipples, and I gripped the sheets tighter, my second orgasm fast approaching.

"Master!" He gripped my hair, pulling my head back.

"Yes, Baby?" His groans were intoxicating. When I only answered with moans, he continued. "Baby, I've needed this. I've heard your moans when my brothers fuck you, and it drove me crazy."

I thought back to the many times I'd fucked one of the others in the next room where he could hear us. Had I caused this? Did the sounds of me having sex drive him to be so sick earlier? My heart dropped as realization hit me. When I fucked Henry this morning. I came down afterwards to find him in the bathroom. How could I have been so stupid as to not see how much worse he got every time I'd fucked? He spanked me again, harder this time, bringing my mind back to the present. "Fuck." I hissed.

"Listen to me, Baby." When he saw he had my attention again, he thrust inside of me and leaned over, kissing my neck. "I don't mind sharing you with them. My brothers and I had several talks the first couple months you were gone, accepting each of us having you. None of us are jealous of the others." He groaned in my ear. "But every time I hear you with them, I want you. Something in me craves your moans, your touch. Fuck, I want all of you." His words hit deep. "We, you and I, still need to talk, but I need you to know, we love you. I love you."

"I love you, too, Drake." He kissed the back of my neck before he started to thrust again, faster, harder, causing me to cum hard around his cock.

"Fuck, I'm going to cum." Drake growled and I whimpered, causing him to pull out and cum on my ass. He collapsed next to me, breathing heavily.

"Feel better?" I asked, looking over at him, smiling.

"Much." He kissed my forehead. "Now, let me get you cleaned up." He carried me to the bathroom before pressing me against the shower wall. "Tell me, Baby, how many times while away did you make yourself cum?"

Fuck, I didn't know, but he expected an answer. "I don't know." How could he expect me to know over the course of two years how many times I came?

He chuckled, confusing me. "I expect the same answer after I ask you about tonight." Drake turned on the shower and held me against the wall, kissing me. My nails raked across his back, riling him up further as he picked me up and shoved his cock inside of me, filling me instantly. My moans silenced by his mouth on mine

"Oh, fuck yes." If this is how he wanted to relieve his excess energy, I would happily oblige, over and over again.

Monday, October 9th, 2017

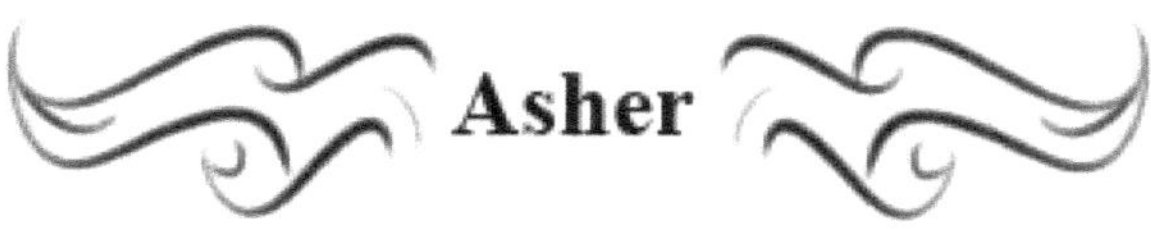

Asher

Asher walked with his brothers back to Amelia's cabin. They'd been out all night doing their rounds of the park while one of them stayed at their house, rotating shifts every so often to see if Lindsay would come back and try something. There'd been a few fallen trees they moved off the trails, but all in all, it was an uneventful night. When the first light of the morning peeked through the trees, they'd decided to head back to the cabin. The doctor did say Drake would need to shift when he woke up. Despite the trust they have that Nick's anti-magic ring would work. It would feel better if they were all together for a flight.

The only thing causing their worries to go down was knowing Amelia would get them if something happened to their brother. When they landed on the property, they shifted back, walking over to the bin of clothes. "Amelia is right, you know," Landon spoke up, breaking the silence. "We need to go after Lindsay once Drake feels better."

"We need to talk to Nick and Mom first." Henry shook his head. "Nick has the most experience dealing with them. He should know how to handle this. I know Amelia is out for blood, and I don't blame her, but there are better ways to go about it."

Asher looked between the twins and thought quietly as they walked to the front door. There was something off about the smell around here, but he couldn't place it; sweet-smelling but with a harsh sting, almost of electricity in the air. It wasn't until he opened the door that the smell was clear as day. His older brothers paused as they looked at the empty pull-out couch. "Upstairs." Asher pointed to Amelia's room. The smell of sex wasn't fresh, maybe an hour or so old. "They're probably sleeping by now, but I don't think we should join in the pile. I don't think he got out all of his energy with that fuck." With his brothers agreeing, they walked out of the cabin and raced to their house.

All three of them stopped, seeing the brunette waiting on the porch, tapping her foot impatiently. "Where the fuck is he?" She yelled, storming down the driveway.

"He's somewhere healing," Landon growled. "Somewhere you can't go."

Lindsay scoffed, stopping in front of them. "He'll have to come out sometime. Whatever you guys think you've done, I'll reverse it back. He's mine, and I plan on keeping it that way."

"What the fuck do you want from him anyway?" Asher asked, calmer than his older brothers but still ready to fight at a moment's notice.

"I want your land, your territory. If I get the alpha, I'll get more territory for my coven." She shrugged. "I'll get more powerful. My position in the coven would surpass even my father. I wouldn't have to answer to anyone I didn't want to."

"Manipulation and mind magic isn't the way to do that." Asher could tell she was getting desperate the longer she stood in front of them.

"It was the only way to go about it! With the four of you looking all over for that bitch, I had to do something, and who better to go after than the alpha? It was all going great; I got more powerful over time, and Drake finally proposed after so much of my magic changing old memories of his. Either way, the bitch is going to get what's coming to her. My father apparently has it out for her, and her family, and he never loses. When she comes out of hiding, he'll come for her." Lindsay walked to her car, twirling her keys around her finger. "Enjoy your precious time while you have it. I'll come back with an army." She drove off, the pink fading off into the distance, while her threat lingered in the air.

"We'll need to ask Nick if he could ward our property like how he has his, so she can't come back." Going inside, they felt the exhaustion of the past 24 hours, and each went to their room to sleep. At least they know one thing. She was after Drake because he was the alpha. If she kept her focus on Drake, who was safe behind Nick's wards, they would all be okay for the time being.

Chapter Eight

Douglas

AMBER BARLOUGH, A SHORT, MIDDLE-AGED woman with blonde hair falling to her hips. She had fallen head over heels for Alvin, her childhood sweetheart. Unfortunately, when he found out about her infertility in their early twenties, he left her and married out of the coven to produce an heir. Heartbroken, she went and found a widower, high-ranking in the coven, who already had a son. Soon, finding herself married to the man, she gained more power than ever. Although she still loved Alven, she was happy with her new life, raising the baby boy, Douglas. Amber bore no resemblance to the black-haired child, but she loved him as if he were her own. The blonde kept in touch with her not-so-secret childhood love, and when she got the recent call from Al, she got giddy with excitement.

Douglas was also delighted that he, once again, had an excuse to see Lindsay. They had a few flings in the past, but she always changed her mind about him just before he'd ask her to come back to live with him. Why she kept deciding to live with her father, he didn't know. Douglas knew all about her father's history of violence and how much of a control freak he could be. Douglas said goodbye to his own father, who was too busy with paperwork to reply. Figures. Rich parents were great until they needed to actually parent, too busy with work to pay attention to those around them, at least, that was his experience.

Amber drew the teleportation runes on the ground, the circle glowing a baby blue. Douglas stepped through the portal, his stepmother's hand on his arm, and arrived in the kitchen of the Divine Sweet Tooth. "They have updated," Douglas commented, looking at the new ovens. It was in the middle of the night, so they wouldn't be turned on for baking for a while. The two newcomers walked up the stairs to the living space of the Hermig residence, walking in as if they owned the place. Alvin looked up from his desk and smiled, walking over to the Blonde.

"Amber, it's been too long." Alvin hugged the woman before kissing both of her cheeks. "Douglas, it's nice to see you again." Shaking hands, Alvin and Douglas had fake smiles plastered on their faces. "I'm glad you could make it on such short notice." They all walked into the living room, the older two sitting on the couch.

"'Is Lindsay upstairs?" Douglas asked, looking around to see what little had changed about this place since the last time he visited.

"She's out right now. I'm sure you'll find her." Alvin waved off the younger male and looked at Amber. "I can confirm the Swallows have moved back into their cabin." At the mention of the last name, Douglas paused to listen. "Unfortunately, it seems Amelia has taken the other dragon shifters to the cabin and is hiding the alpha." It made the young man's blood boil. That family has caused nothing but trouble for his coven, keeping his father busy and away from him. He has never met a dragon, let alone a dragon shifter, but with everything he has heard, nothing good could come from them. Dragon shifters were selfish and relentless, destroying anything and everything around them.

Without further listening to the conversation his mother and Alvin were having, he closed his eyes and concentrated, moving his hands, drawing runes in the air, and whispered an incantation.

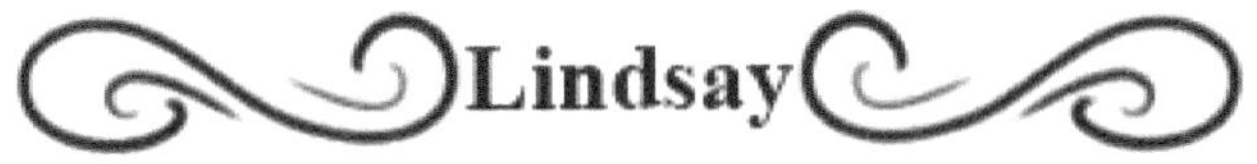

It had been days of looking for Drake in this damned forest with no luck. Driving to yet another trail, Lindsay sped down the road. With only a small woosh of air being her warning, Douglas teleported into her car, sitting in the passenger seat. "Holy fucking Hells!" Lindsay yelled, the car swerving, but Douglas guided the car back quickly into the proper lane with a wave of his hand. Lindsay glared at the man now in her car. "No fucking warning?! No voices in my head saying you're on your way?" Lindsay hit his chest, hoping to leave a painful mark.

"I apologize, my lady." He smiled at her. "I had been irritated by the mention of what brought me here in the first place, not that I do not absolutely adore visiting you, Dear."

Lindsay rolled her eyes. "Don't get me started. I need to find out where this cabin is, and how to get there, so I can get my shit back on track."

"Do not bother, Sweetheart." He relaxed, leaning the seat back. "You will be crawling to the door if you get that far. You have no idea what it is like to not have magic. Not just to have no access to your magic but to have all of your magic sucked out of your very existence. Your muscles will get weak without the energy surging through your veins." He looked at the woman and admired her. "You should smile, be happy. You are prettier when you smile, Dove."

"Yeah? And you should fuck off. I have every right to be pissed off right now." She glared at the road. Lindsay hadn't slept in what felt like days, only getting in a couple of hour naps here and there in her car. That alpha was her only way out of her father's influence, but the chances were looking worse as the days sped by.

"I can assist you." He leaned over and put a hand on her thigh. "You know I will." He squeezed, trying to reassure her, but every time he touched her, she felt as if he was messing with her mind.

Lindsay batted away the hand and forced it back in his own lap. "I don't need your help, thank you very much. I'd rather do it myself." If he helped her, he'd get most of the credit she deserved. He'd get the title boost, though it's not like he needed it with his father being who he was. No, this was her problem, and she would fix it on her own. It didn't matter that she told Drake's brothers she'd bring more people, knowing it would be Douglas and his mother coming. He was not what she needed right now. She only said it to make them on edge and make some mistake to reveal where the fucking cabin was.

"Hey." Douglas looked at her. "You do not have to, is what I am trying to convey. Look, Gorgeous, I will help you take out the Swallow girl and her uncle. They will be out of your hair in no time. I will do it with great prejudice." He spoke darkly, wanting to rid the world of dragon shifters. His hands started to glow black as he clenched his fists.

Lindsay raised an eyebrow. "Is that all you'd help with?" It wouldn't be too bad if he helped get rid of the bitch in her way.

"Is there something else you need help with, Lovely?"

"No," Lindsay said too quickly.

"Come on, Babe. You can tell me. Is there something else you need assistance with?" He raised an eyebrow and turned in his seat slightly to look at her more.

"I don't need help with it, especially not your help. And stop with the pet names." She parked in the back of her family's bakery with the apartment above. "Where are you staying while visiting?" She knew the answer already, but hoped she was wrong.

Douglas smirked at her. "Where do you think? My mother will conjure her bed in the living room for the night, and I will be sharing your bed." It was the way they always did it, no matter how much Lindsay voiced her protests with her father or Douglas about it. There was no arguing with her father when his mind was made up.

"How long are you both going to stay?" she asked begrudgingly. It didn't matter that the two of them could teleport every day. Her father's argument was always that it was more convenient for them to sleep at our place.

"As long as it takes to get rid of those damned shifters." His mood shifted as he spoke. "Dragons do not need to roam the earth."

"Not all shifters are bad. Some can be used to gain power." She locked the car and the two walked up to the apartment silently before tiptoeing through the living room where Amber slept. When they got to her room, she went straight to her desk while Douglas went to her bed, lying above the covers. Pulling out one of her spell books, she started reading, studying the text she memorized years ago. It was the spell book she'd copied from her father when she was young. A few pages turned on their own, much to her displeasure. "Can I help you? I'm trying to study."

"You will not get anything new from reading that old thing again. If you want, I can help you study," he said seductively and winked. "Come here." With another wiggle of his fingers, his uncomfortable-looking suit was replaced with a pair of black silk pajamas.

Instead of doing what he wanted, she threw the magic-laced book at him. "Go fuck off somewhere. I didn't ask for your help, nor do I need it. I don't want your help."

Douglas shook his head. "What you need is rest. Come to bed; I will assist you in the morning." He moved the blanket to the side before moving himself under it.

Lindsay could feel the pull he put in her mind and fought it; the past couple of years had helped her gain more of her mental fortitude. Dealing with an alpha's presence was no small feat. "Stop it. I will not have you control me." He nodded his head at her, impressed. Telling herself she didn't need his approval, she turned in her chair, summoned her spell book back to her hands, and continued reading.

"Have it your way. Come to bed when you are ready." She glanced at him, and he made himself comfortable, closing his eyes to sleep. Good, the less of his voice she had to listen to, the better. It was about an hour later, when she was sure he was asleep and wouldn't try anything, that Lindsay dared get into bed, sleeping on the edge, as far away from him as possible.

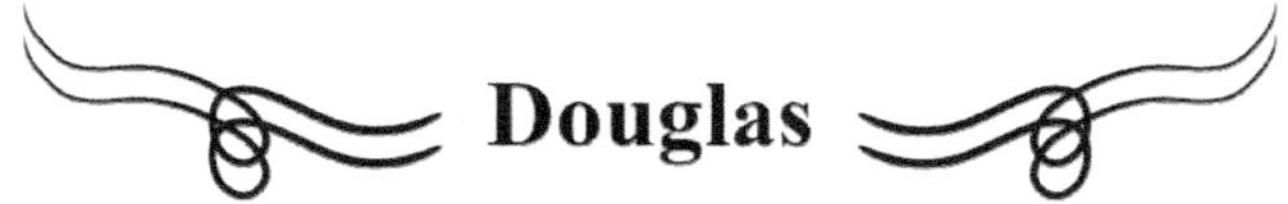

Douglas

Waiting for her to come to bed was the hard part. He would even subtly cast an illusion spell to make it seem as though he was in a deep slumber when she was concentrating hard on one of the spells she read. As he lay there, he thought about what she said on their way here, becoming ever confused by her meaning. What power was to be gained by a low-life such as a dragon? He needed to do some more digging into what they were capable of. Being the son of a high-ranking member of the coven, Douglas had more access to resources than others like Lindsay, but he would help her out and give her an old spell book of his with new spells and techniques that were new to her.

There were rules about the distribution of power among the Sliver of Divinity. Everything had to be earned, and it didn't matter who you stepped on to get it. He could see that Lindsay was the epitome of that idea growing in power since he had last seen her. What had it been, a year and a half, almost two years now? Douglas had been too busy, caught up in the Southwestern United States under his father's orders. He would stay at his home in Seattle to sleep but teleport to where he needed to be during waking hours, most recently spending a few weeks in Colorado near the Four Corners searching for Fae.

When Lindsay finally came to bed, lying as far away from him as possible, he waited until she was asleep, which, thankfully, did not take long. Muttering to himself an incantation, he placed two fingers on her forehead and closed his eyes.

When he opened his eyes, he was next to a lake and saw Lindsay running, laughing. It brought a smile to his face until he saw she was running towards a blonde male. He walked closer, and the two kissed, infuriating him. Ethereal red fire emanated from around his closed fists. She was his and belonged to no one else. As he got closer, they separated, and when Lindsay saw him, she held onto the male closer. Douglas saw a female appear next to him with wavy brown hair. "What the Hell is going on?" He asked, stomping closer, pulling the couple apart from one another, the woman beside him pulling the male away as he pulled Lindsay.

"You can't have him anymore," The woman beside him yelled. "He's no longer under your spells. He can see right through you." This angered Lindsay, and she waved her hand, a puff of smoke coming from her hands as she had tried to cast but was unable to. Douglas found she was often unable to cast in her dreams, finding it similar to dreams where people could not run fast or punch hard.

"Lindsay," Douglas tried to get through to her, to take her attention away from the woman who helped him separate the two. "Who are these two?" His words seeped into her innermost thoughts as she fought his control.

Her reply was forced out of her as she tried not to speak, making her voice sound strangled. "Drake and Amelia."

It surprised him that, even in her unconscious state, Lindsay could fight his influence now. "That is their names, but who are they to you?"

Lindsay grabbed her head as she tried to resist answering him. "He's my tool for power, and she's trying to stop me." Tears rolled down her cheeks as she looked up at him. "You are the one who's going to steal the credit from me."

Douglas stepped back at the accusation she spat at him. It was then that it clicked in his mind that those two behind him were dragon shifters. He got angry, and the environment around them changed. "You laid with a dragon? When all you had to do was accept that I am trying to help you by taking you away from your father? That is what you have been doing for the past two years here?" Dark energy surrounded his form. "I am going to kill them. I am going to kill all of them."

Chapter Nine

Thursday, October 12th, 2017

Amelia

WAKING UP IN MY BED AT THE WINDSOR'S place, I groaned at the unpleasant ray of sunlight shining in my eyes from the small space between the curtains. Rolling to the side, I put an arm out, surprised not to feel another body next to me. All four boys had slept in the bed with me last night. At least one of them should have been here, unless something went wrong. Sitting up, panic coursed through my veins as I looked around to find I was alone. Jumping out of bed, not caring about my unclad form, I ran downstairs, calling out for my men. "Drake!" No answer. "Henry!" Nothing. "Lany!" My calls became more desperate as I reached the second story. "Asher!" Silence. If they were here, they should have heard me and called back to me. I barged into the closest room. First, Drake's room. Empty. Asher's room. Empty. Next was Henry's office. No one was in there either. The next room I checked was the gaming room. All four of the brothers were hooked up to their own VR setup. Asher was the first one to take off the headset, and he immediately unhooked the rest of the sensors before he ran to me. Relief overwhelmed me, and I fell to my knees, unable to hold steady. The floor was nice. It would hold me up. The cold sensation helping me ground myself in reality. My boys are okay. I am okay. Now, if only I could convince my body of those facts.

"What's wrong?" He hugged me tightly. The next one beside me was Landon, whose VR setup was the closest. The feeling of relief took some time to process. Adrenaline still pulsed through my body as the conflicting emotions overwhelmed me. Tears freely fell onto Asher's shirt as I reassured myself that my boys are safe. I am safe.

"Did something happen?" Drake asked, anger threaded through his words at the possibility of me getting hurt.

Shaking my head, I looked at the four of them. "No."

"Bad dream?" Henry asked, putting a hand through my hair. I chose that feeling to focus on, grateful for it

I once again shook my head. "I thought something happened… I woke up and no one was there." Saying it out loud made me feel foolish. There were plenty of times when I'd woken up alone before I disappeared to Arizona, and I was fine then. Taking a deep breath, I looked around. Concern was written all over their faces. "I'm sorry. I shouldn't have worried." I was stupid. We were okay. I shouldn't have had such an extreme reaction to waking up alone.

"Don't ever apologize for your true feelings, especially if they're that powerful." Drake kissed my forehead.

I nodded, but it didn't change my thought process. "I'll get dressed and then make some breakfast." My voice betrayed me, causing Asher to tighten his hold.

"Mom already did that." He calmly whispered in my ear, though all of the occupants in the room could hear him. "Do you want one of us to go with you?"

"No." There was no need, really. They were all safe right now. "You guys keep playing your game." I smiled, but it didn't reach my eyes. I knew, with the years of missed bonding time, the brothers needed it.

Henry walked over, wordlessly, to his VR setup and logged his character out. "You're still shaken up. I'll help." He smiled at the other three. "We'll be back." He put his arm around me, and Asher let go, taking a step back.

Sitting on my bed, having just put on some plaid boy shorts. Henry sat next to me, an arm around my shoulders. "It's all right. Ya know? To worry about us. None of us let you know where we were or that none of us would be here when you woke up." His voice soothed me, almost cutting through my inner voice. Almost.

"I acted irrationally. I just," Pausing, thinking about what to say, I was unsure how to voice what I felt, the words not coming to mind quickly. "I just panicked. I thought…" How do I say I thought my coming back was all just a dream, and I thought I was hallucinating being back in the Windsor manner? That it wouldn't have been the first time if I were hallucinating. "I thought something went terribly wrong." Shaking my head at how stupid my actions were, I continued. "I shouldn't have, though. If something was wrong, one of you would have woken me up when you left," I rationalized out loud. Henry kissed my forehead. "Thank you for taking care of me." Kissing his bare chest, I cuddled closer to him. While I know my boys worried they would lose me, I had to reassure myself I wasn't dreaming or hallucinating being back.

"No need for thanks." He squeezed me before letting go and standing up. With a dramatic bow at the hips, Henry looked up at me. "Anything you wish for is yours. I am your humble servant."

Giggling, I blushed at his antics. "You've always been one for the dramatics." I put a hand out for him, and he grabbed it, pulling me off the bed to stand so my chest was pressed against his.

"Would you want me any other way?" His voice sounded huskier with every syllable he spoke.

"Not at all." The kiss was slow, filled with deep understanding. The moment was cut short, however, when my stomach growled, reminding me how I needed breakfast.

Henry was the one to pull away, concerned about my recent eating habits, or lack thereof. "You should eat." I cursed inwardly at my damned starving stomach. These moments needed to last longer. I missed too much in the past two years. I needed these sweet moments. I fucking deserved them.

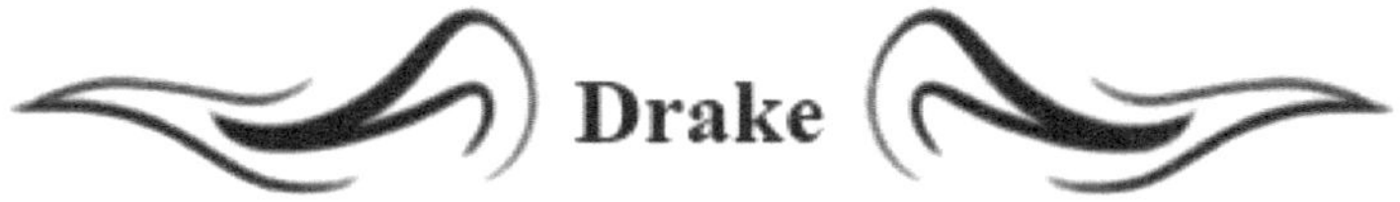 Drake

After agreeing to speak with Nick about how Amelia reacted today and confirming with a text to Nick that he was home, Drake raced his youngest brother on foot to the Swallow's cabin while Landon stayed back. Drake looked back to see how far ahead he was and, to his surprise, Asher was just beyond his peripheral vision, behind him. A smile came to Drake as he thought about sparring with his brother. He couldn't remember the last time they did so. The Alpha hated how much the mage, Lindsay, messed with his mind, making him believe his brothers were awful. With the memories he'd been able to separate as real vs conjured, Drake did go out on the search for Amelia with his brothers twice a week, but before they left and after he came back, she'd distort his memories.

"Watch out, I might beat you," Asher said, teasingly.

"Right, and I'm the queen of England." Drake quickened his pace, but so did Asher, keeping on his heels. Drake narrowed his eyes as he looked forward, a blue glimmer of something appearing in the distance, a vertical line in the middle of the road forming out from nowhere. It opened to reveal a man, dressed in a black suit and tie with a bright red dress shirt. Once the man stepped out of the shimmering blue light, he put a hand up, and a wall of ice appeared just in front of the two brothers, causing them both to slam into it and fall back. "Fuck." Drake rubbed his head, propping himself up on one hand. Asher growled and slowly stood, trying the walk-it-off tactic. The dark-haired man walked towards them slowly, the wall not going away, but slowly shifting from being clouded to clear ice. Through the slightly warped image of the man, the brothers couldn't make out much, but knew by his scent, they'd never met before.

"Are you Drake Windsor?" The man called out, adjusting his suit jacket.

"Yeah, and you are?" Drake stood, wiping off the slight mud that got on his jeans.

With another wave of the man's hands, the ice wall vaporized, causing the humidity to rise and the temperature to drop around them slightly for a few moments. The shorter, dark-haired man looked Drake up and down before looking at Asher the same way. "And you are?" The disdain was prominent in his voice.

"Answer Drake's question first." Asher crossed his arms.

"Very well, if you must know." He rolled his eyes and looked at the blonde. "My name is Douglas Barlough." His eyes lingered slightly, eyeing Drake's build. Jealousy bubbled in his chest, and he wondered if that was why Lindsay thought she would gain power by marrying this… thing. His eyes turned to the younger man. "Now it is your turn."

"Asher." Asher let his arms down to put a hand in his pocket. Grabbing his phone, he pressed and held one of the side buttons, speed-dialing the manor.

"A dragon, too, I suspect?" Douglas raised an eyebrow. Without any confirmation, he continued. "Might as well be with how uncivilized you all are." He spoke as if he were almost bored with the interaction.

"Uncivilized? You're the one who put up the ice wall and didn't introduce yourself first." Asher growled, but Drake held his hand out to stop his brother.

"What is it that you want?" Though suspicious, Drake didn't feel the need to use his alpha presence yet.

Douglas ignored the younger dragon and smirked at Drake. "I want to know what power you possess that you were going to give to my love."

The brothers looked at each other, confused, and then back at the man. "What?" They asked, simultaneously.

Douglas sighed. "I'll force it out of your mind if I must. I also want to know how you were going to give her such powers. Do you have books you were holding from her? Enchanted items, perhaps?"

"Dude, I have no idea what you're talking about," Drake said with complete honesty. "Or who you're talking about, for starters."

"Lindsay, your betrothed, the love of my life, brown hair, blue eyes, about four-foot nine, give or take a half inch depending on the time of day." He put his hand out about a foot shorter than him for emphasis.

"The one who had me under a spell for the better part of the last two years?" Drake couldn't help the smoke from blowing out of his nose as his anger rose. "I can't say that I know what you're talking about, but if you associate with her, you need to leave. Now." He put emphasis on the last word, allowing some of his alpha presence to seep in to have more of an effect.

"So, you do have something in you. Otherwise, I would not have felt such intimidation. Maybe she never told you and was simply holding out until she found a way to extract whatever that was from you." He rubbed his hairless chin in thought. "I will admit, I don't know too much about your anatomy or how your magic works, and I will have to do some digging," he paused as he took a step back, "but rest assured, Drake, I will be back, and when I am, you will not be the same." He waved his hands and said a small incantation before he disappeared, the sliver of glimmering light appearing in his place. It too dispersed into the air after mere moments, and the brothers stood there, stunned.

"Who the Hells does he think he is?" Asher growled. "If he thinks that he'll be back and we will just roll over onto our bellies like scared little wyrmlings, he's got another thing coming."

Drake put a hand on his brother's shoulder, smiling slightly. "Don't worry. You won't lose me again. We'll bring this up to Nick when we get there. Let's not have this ruin our day. We knew that she'd show up again sometime. At least we know she's outsourcing and the name of who she's got." He spoke calmly, hoping his brother would follow suit.

Asher took a few deep breaths and nodded. "You're right." He pulled his phone out of his pocket. "Hello?" He asked, seeing that someone from the house had picked up the phone.

"Is everything okay? I couldn't make out much." Landon asked.

"Yeah. Everything is alright. I do think it would be better for you guys to meet us at Nick's. We have a newcomer in town and he ain't friendly." Asher and Drake walked forward but were on high alert for anything off around them.

"Okay. I'll grab the other two."

Nick sat on the front porch, reading a book his father had sent him to learn more about enchantment and illusion magics, when Drake and Asher came running onto the property. "What's got you two in a rush?"

"Well, we were coming to talk with you about something that happened this morning, but now we have even more to discuss," Drake sighed, leaning against the railing, sliding his hand down his face.

"Is it about Lindsay?" The older shifter closed the book after putting a receipt in it as a bookmark.

"Kinda?" Asher tilted his head to the side, unsure of how to verbalize the new problem.

"The other three are on their way and should be here in no time. Asher and I had a run-in with a guy we'd never met. By the way he was talkin', we believe he's involved with Lindsay. I can't tell for sure, though, because he said some confusing things." Drake took out his phone to text the Doc to meet at the Swallow's.

"Were you followed?" Nick stood, taking a look behind them.

"Not that we could detect. The guy left almost as quickly as he came. It was weird, magics I've never seen before, and he didn't really attack us, more like..." Asher scratched the back of his head. "He wanted to introduce himself to us."

"We should wait until the others get here to explain more." Drake walked inside and sat on the couch. Just being in this house, he was feeling calmer.

Amelia

Walking down to the kitchen, I saw Lany hang up the landline. "What's up?" I didn't like the confused and concerned look he had.

"Drake and Asher went to go talk with Nick at your place and," He paused, making my mind start to think of the worst. "They are alright." Lany put a hand out, halting the rising panic I felt in my chest. "They did meet a new fella, and we need to meet at your place to talk."

To talk. I hadn't had the talk I knew I needed to have with my men. The longer I took to tell them, the worse I felt about it. I didn't intentionally hide it, but I also couldn't bring myself to talk about it. Fuck, it hurt to say "it". He? She? I didn't know, and I wasn't able to find out.

"Amelia?" Henry put his hand on my shoulder. "Are you okay?" Looking up at the only one who knew, I nodded. It was time.

"I'll race ya." Before I could book it out the front door, Henry's hand squeezed my shoulder.

"We will grab some of the food Mom made us and take it so you will eat." He had a point, and Lany looked at my stomach as it growled again at the mention of food.

Just as the two Windsors and I walked onto my property, I saw the luxury SUV pull in, and Doctor Logan rolled down the window. "Is everything okay?"

"That's what they tell me." I took a bite of my waffle. The blonde nodded and drove up the rest of the way to the cabin.

When we walked in, I saw Mable sitting on the couch with Uncle Nick and Drake. Asher sat on the loveseat next to the Doc, and I sat on Lany's lap as he sat in the recliner, while Henry stood next to where Mable sat. "You said something happened this morning." Uncle Nick started the conversation, causing me to blush in embarrassment. I was so stupid this morning. That's all it was, my stupidity. Couldn't we all accept it and get past it? Forget about it?

"It was nothing," I reassured them. I knew it was nothing. It was just my mind playing tricks on me.

"It wasn't nothing." Drake looked at me pointedly.

"We are worried about you, Amelia," Henry added.

Lany rubbed my arm to try to reassure me. "Did something happen to cause that reaction?"

"What did happen?" Uncle Nick questioned.

"I…" Taking a deep breath, I found a place in the ground to find fascinating. "It's nothing, really. I just panicked a little when I woke up. No one was hurt."

"It didn't look like nothing." Asher's concern tore at my heart. "You were about to go into a panic attack."

"What triggered it?" I knew where Uncle Nick was going to go with his line of questioning. I was put on anxiety meds six months after my accident, and, although they helped, I didn't want to be on meds again. I was fine. I am fine, just the way I am. Nothing is wrong with me.

"She was alone when she woke up and thought something had happened." I looked at Henry as he spoke, needing the comfort of someone who knew what I was feeling.

"Did something happen while you were away to cause you to panic like that?" Drake questioned. I couldn't look at him, at any of them, so I looked at the floor again, knowing I looked guilty as Hell. After a few silent moments, Drake spoke again, more concerned. "Amelia?"

My hand went to my abdomen as I tried to form the words to say what I needed to. "It's hard to talk about." Landon put his arms around me to comfort me. It took several deep breaths for the words to come out. "I was… pregnant when I, when we," I pointed between Uncle Nick and myself with my thumb and pinky, "disappeared." I saw the confusion in Drake's eyes and felt Landon's arms loosen from around me slightly. Asher looked dumbfounded, not knowing how to process the information. Deep breath in, deep breath out. "I had a miscarriage." Closing my eyes, I tried not to go back,

168

not to be in the hospital again. Putting my hand on Landon's knee, I moved my thumb to focus on the feeling of the present. His jeans were rough but not uncomfortably so.

"What… what happened?" Asher's voice was a whisper, but everyone in the room heard him. Even Doctor Logan looked over at him before looking at me for the story.

"My aunt and I were attacked." Uncle Nick helped me tell the story of how I was attacked and how I found out in the hospital. The further into the story I got, the harder it was to form words, watching the emotions I felt flash through my boys' eyes. Anger, hurt, betrayal, mourning, realization, and sadness were all there, cycling through each of them. There was no changing the past, though, no going back, hoping to change things. By the end of the story, all of my boys had tears flowing down their cheeks and moved closer to me, either sitting at my feet or standing next to me with the exception of Landon, who I was sitting on. I could see blood slowly trickle from Asher's hands as his claws dug into his palms. Mable had started crying into Uncle Nick's shoulder as we all felt the loss of what could have been.

"They are dead, or at least, the ones who participated in the attack are. They were, apparently, a part of the Sliver of Divinity."

"Speaking of them." Asher looked over at his oldest brother.

"On our way over here, we were stopped by a man. Said his name was Douglas Barlough." I saw Uncle Nick tense at the name.

"You know him?" I asked. How much did Uncle Nick know, that he wasn't telling me?

"I've never heard of Douglas, but I have heard of a man with the Sliver of Divinity who goes by George Barlough. He's the head of the Barlough family, the man I picture when I think of the coven." He rubbed his forehead as he sighed and leaned back. "The Barlough family has been the leader of the coven for generations. He's not a friendly face, especially when dragons are involved."

"Dragon shifters," Logan corrected, "I doubt he knows about actual dragons."

"What do you mean, actual dragons?" Did he think we were somehow fake dragons? I shift and I become a dragon. Anger started to bubble inside of me as I realized we knew almost nothing about this doctor and, yes, he saved Drake's life, but who did he think he was? "We shift into actual dragons." I was about to tear him a new one when he put a hand up, defensively.

"Yes, I'm not saying you don't. I'm talking about the dragon souls, with soul bonds." I understood he was saying words, but they made no sense. He looked at all of us, but realized none of us understood what he was talking about. "You five," He cleared his throat before looking at Mable and Uncle Nick, "seven, are dragon shifters." He seemed to stumble over his words before shaking his head. Wait, was the doctor not a dragon shifter? What else was out there? As I was about to ask more, He continued speaking. "Look, there's a lot to unpack with that, and we have bigger issues at the moment." He looked at Nick. "Please, continue."

"Anywho… I'm sure this Douglas fellow would be his son. If Lindsay is working under their orders, we have a bigger fight than I originally thought. Thankfully, my sister has finally agreed to visit and bring with her some more research on the coven, and should be here tomorrow. She will also be helping me ward the Windsor estate."

At the mention of my Aunt Carol, I perked up. I missed the woman who became my best friend for the past two years. Doubts seeped into my mind when I realized she wouldn't be here until tomorrow. "What are we going to do between now and then? What if any of us have another run-in with Douglas, or what if George shows up?" What if George is already here? The more I spoke, the faster my words came out. I wasn't afraid of Lindsay, but it seemed as though she was bringing in the big guns

"Lindsay," I growled, everything adding up. She was the reason my life has been a living nightmare. Whether it be her specifically or her family or the Barloughs, I no longer cared. She was going to die, and it would be by my hand. I'd have to catch her while she was alone, weak. Drake rubbed my arm, bringing me back to the present. "I'm going to kill her."

"I won't stop you when it's the right time. However, now is not the time. There are too many unknowns."

"What if the Barloughs are stronger than we can fend off?" We needed backup. My aunt is coming tomorrow, but what about my cousins? I had another aunt and uncle who had several children who had land not too far away from my grandfather. What would happen if they left Arizona to come and fight here? Would that leave an opening for the coven to attack whoever stays behind? We were strong in numbers, but would so many of my family leaving there to come help us raise too much suspicion? Too many thoughts wracked through my brain, and Asher scoffed. Landon chuckled, and I felt like I missed something by being too much in my head.

"Lia, there's nothing we can't handle when we're all together." Landon kissed the back of my shoulder and smirked against my skin. "We just stick together, and everything will be okay." He rubbed my hair softly. With all of my boys around me, reassuring me, I felt invincible. Landon was right; nothing was ever going to separate my boys from me again.

Chapter Ten

Friday, October 13th, 2017

HELPING MABLE SET THE DINING ROOM table, I looked out the window for the umpteenth time. "Hon, if you watch the water, it'll never boil." Mable nodded at me and then at the window as she placed the last glass in her hand down.

"They should be here any minute. Her plane landed almost two hours ago." I put a fork on the folded napkin, following the wiser woman back to the kitchen, where the smell of pork chops was calling my name.

"And your Uncle is a responsible driver without a carsick passenger who didn't live here almost her whole life. Maybe your aunt wanted to stop and smell the roses." Knowing my aunt, she probably did want to stop and look at all the wonderful scenery.

"Good morning, Mom." Henry chimed as he walked in and wrapped his arm around my waist.

"Oh, good, you can start helping me with the Omelets." Mable smiled and took out the eggs. Henry left my side to help his mother, but the warmth at my side was quickly replaced when Asher wrapped his arm around my shoulder.

"Asher." Without looking to see who had walked in, Mable knew. "We just finished setting the table. Would you set out the drinks?" Mable took a step away from the fridge and started whisking the eggs.

"Yes, ma'am." Asher moved to the coffee pot to start the coffee.

"Good Morning, Lia." Lany kissed my forehead, and I giggled, knowing he'd be put to work by Mable also. Like clockwork, Lany was instructed on setting out the seasonings on the table.

Knowing I had already done my portion of the work by setting the table with Mable, I took a few steps back and walked to the living room to see Drake sitting on the couch. "Hey." I smiled, sitting down next to him. "Didn't want to be put to work?"

"I'm doing my job." He smirked and moved me to straddle his lap.

"You are?"

"Yes. I'm to keep you distracted so you're not worrying yourself to death." His hands fell to my hips, and I looked back at the hallway.

"How do you plan on doing that?" While I was not opposed to fucking within earshot of his brothers, Mable was a different story.

"Tell me about Arizona." He tilted his head curiously, as if studying my reaction.

"It's hot. Or, at least it can be. Where I was, it wasn't too miserable." At his chuckle, I got confused. "What?"

"I meant, what did you do? People you met. I didn't ask about the weather."

"Oh, well, over there, when you ask about how someone or something is, weather is one of the first things brought up." I rubbed my abdomen. "I lived with my grandpa, Harold. He's Nick's dad. My aunt Carol also lived in the house, but I had a few other aunts and uncles who lived not too far away from my grandpa's property. There wasn't much I did other than have my aunt teach me more about partial shifting."

That last part was a lie, and he knew it. I thought about the 5 months I spent on my own. "It was after I got out of the hospital." I placed my head on his chest, and one of his hands started slowly rubbing my back in soothing circles. "I was so angry at everything and everyone." Though I whispered into his chest, I knew he could hear me as evidenced by his tightening grip around me. "I was scared."

"What happened?"

"I ran. I had a half-assed plan to find those mages who killed my… our child. My aunt, Carol, had been studying them. I read only a few things, but once I got my lead as to where to look, I didn't care about waiting anymore. I packed my bags that night and ran. I was in Strawberry at the time and headed to Tucson. It's a bit longer than from here to Nashville and a whole lot deader, but the mountains were pretty." I chuckled but then sighed, knowing I'd have to continue. "I know it was stupid to go off on my own. I don't need any more lectures on that, but I didn't know if or when I'd be allowed back here, and I'd just lost the only thing of y'all's I had left. I spent about five months on my own, and I picked the wrong five months in Arizona. Long story short, they weren't in Tucson when I arrived, and I spent until May there before I learned about their base in Yuma from overhearing these two guys in the middle of a burger joint.

At first, when I overheard the two guys, I thought they were talking about a book, but the longer they talked, the more I believed they knew about the coven I was trying to find, and I'd learned my lesson. As I ate my burger, I learned more about where they were going. It wasn't hard to interject myself into the conversation. I created a sob story about how I needed to get back to Yuma and didn't have any way to get there. I hated how treeless and empty it was there. It made it so much harder to travel in my dragon form. With about an hour's worth of conversation, they agreed to take me with them in exchange for gas.

I asked why they still drove a gas-powered vehicle, but the owner of the beaten-up old car explained, in great detail, why he couldn't afford a new vehicle and emphasized that it was because the other man kept spending his money. It was about halfway that we stopped, and I got car sick. The guy

176

who supposedly kept spending the car owner's money gave me an anti-nausea pill, and though they don't typically work for me, I was good for the rest of the ride." I sat up so I could look Drake in the eyes. "I don't think they were dragon shifters, but I don't think they were human either. I didn't bring it up, though."

Drake chuckled. "How does one casually ask two guys they just met if they are human or not? If they are, they'd think you're psycho."

"Exactly. Anyway, it took another two months to find their base. Unfortunately, I went in storms a blazing, and got caught. My Aunt Carol found me just as they put me in their holding cell, and it was utter chaos." I stopped as I recalled everything that went on. "There were so many things happening at once. I…" I teared up. "Someone isn't alive today because of me." I shook my head. "I know I shouldn't feel this way, but I'm glad. I saw him and recognized him as one of those who attacked my aunt and me originally. I killed him for killing our baby." Anger flooded me, but I could tell Drake was influencing my emotions by helping keep my anger in check.

"The things they said when they were detaining me, Drake." Those words echoed in my head. "They told me I didn't deserve to live. I didn't deserve anything but pain. I deserved to have nothing." Taking a deep breath, I looked down. "I deserve a family, Drake." I stood up and started to pace as I tried to hold back my anger, but I was allowed to feel anger. "It's not that I don't love the family I have, but I'm allowed to mourn the loss of the family I wasn't able to have. It's not all I want in life, but damn it!" I wrapped my arms around myself. "I love Mable, but what if I want a hug from *my* parents? What if I want to hold my baby in my arms? I can't, but I deserve to have it!" My body was shaking with anger. I could hear the noise in the kitchen stop.

Drake stood slowly before hugging me tightly. "It hurts, Amelia. It hurts that I never got to have that experience with you. It hurts that I can't hold our baby either." He spoke in soft tones. I heard his words clearer than ever. I had someone to sympathize with. For the first time, it truly hit me that my boys felt the exact same way about our loss. It wasn't just the loss of my baby. It was the loss of our baby. I felt more warmth around me as the other three Windsor men walked in, creating a group hug. This was a step towards healing, acknowledging all of our pain, of our loss. "A parent shouldn't have to bury their child."

We stood like that for as long as we could. It wasn't until the sound of a car in the driveway that we broke apart. "That sounds like your aunt is here." Henry broke our silence.

"Breakfast is ready!" Mable called out.

"Just in time, too." Asher chimed.

I rushed to the front yard to meet my Aunt at the car. "Aunt Carol!" She used the car as support to keep standing when I practically tackled her.

"Oh, I missed you!" my aunt exclaimed, squeezing me tighter. "Are those the gods that you couldn't shut up about?" My aunt asked, looking up to see my four men standing on the front porch. She didn't bother to lower her voice, making all four young Windsors smirk at me.

"Aunt Carol," I grumbled as I lightly hit the black-haired woman's arm. "I didn't call them gods. They don't need that ego boost." I smirked back at my boys. "And besides, they bleed. Gods don't bleed." I turned, hearing Doctor Chester's truck pull up.

"How would you know if gods bleed or not? Have you ever met any?" Landon playfully asked, the brothers walking towards us to greet my aunt.

"No. I just know, they wouldn't be gods if they bled." I put my hands on my hips to help make my point. "Then you could kill them."

"You're not entirely correct," Logan spoke up as he got out of the truck. "They can't exactly die, you've got that correct, but they can bleed." Everyone looked at him quizzically.

Before he could clarify, Mable yelled from the front door. "Y'all best get in here if you still want your breakfast warm." Seeing everyone starting to make their way inside, she headed into the kitchen, continuing her cooking of omelets for the newcomers. We all quickly filed in and formed a line. The Windsor boys already had their omelets on their plates, and Mable plated mine as I stepped into the kitchen. "Sides are in the dining room on warming plates, and so are the pork chops. Thank you, boys." Mable smiled and nodded at her sons. "I would take it; you're the woman who kept Amelia sane these past two years?" Mable's warm gaze landed on Carol. "Thank you for taking such good care of her."

"There were some trying times," She smiled at me. "But it was all worth it."

"Honey," Mable chuckled. "There are always trying times; it just matters how much you want to try in those times. How do you take your omelet?"

Landon nudged my shoulder to get my attention and gestured to the dining room. I followed him to see Drake and Doctor Chester sitting down. "What were you saying about gods earlier?" I asked, but was once again interrupted when Uncle Nick walked in.

"Carol said she'd take me car shopping later. Did you want to join?" Uncle Nick sat down at one end of the table.

"No. I'd rather not shop for a woozy death trap, thank you."

"I didn't think so, but I thought I'd ask." Asher and Henry sat down across from me, with Asher next to Doctor Chester and Henry next to the empty seat for Aunt Carol. "You didn't want an omelet, Logan?"

"No, but thank you. I will take one of these pork chops, though."

"Dig right in." Mable sat down at the other end of the table, opposite Nick, with Drake to her right and Doctor Chester to her left.

"What, no potatoes?" Uncle Nick asked as I passed him the hot sauce.

Carol's eyes widened at the question, and backhanded his shoulder. "You want potatoes, you get in there and make them." She scolded her brother.

180

"That's not necessary." Mable chuckled. "Only a few are allowed to cook in my kitchen, and Nick isn't one of them." My boys and I all burst out laughing at remembering the last time Nick was allowed to cook in Mable's kitchen. How he hadn't burned the house down, we had no idea. The fire alarm had gone off several times, and the clean-up took the rest of the day, with everyone helping to clean. It confused the Hells out of me because he could cook and often did at our house, but bad things happened when Nick used Mable's kitchen. "There are small chunks of potato in your omelet." She pointed with her fork. Nick smiled in gratitude before he started eating.

"So, how do you know gods can bleed?" Drake asked, pointing his fork in the doc's direction.

Logan swallowed before smiling. "I've met a couple." I was glad I just swallowed the orange juice I was drinking. Orange juice out of the nose wouldn't have been pleasant. Glancing at the others, I noticed I wasn't the only one who felt that way. Everyone else at the table having paused in their own conversation and looked at him as if he were crazy. "When you've been around for as long as I have, it can happen."

"How long have you been around?" I asked reflexively.

"Only two hundred fifty-four years, give or take, depending on how you spin it."

"Excuse me?" I asked, sure, I heard the wrong number. The doctor didn't look any older than his early thirties. As I looked around again, it surprised me that Drake and my aunt

Carol were the only ones who seemed shocked at the news of the doctor's age.

"You heard me right." The doctor smiled before clearing his throat to quickly change the subject. "Have we had any contact from the coven yet?"

"No. Thank God," I sighed. "Or... thank the gods?" I paused as I contemplated my words. "Wow, now my whole belief system has been called into question." I put my fork down on the plate and stared at the food.

"Well, in my talkings with the few gods I have met, they did speak of an even higher power." Logan leaned forward and spoke thoughtfully. "Though they refused to describe it in any physical form. You can still believe in that higher power as your God."

Henry swallowed before speaking. "But the gods you've met, they still call themselves gods?"

"Yeah. Wouldn't you, if you had that much power?"

"Okay," I shrugged. "But if something can bleed, it can die. You said they can't die."

Logan chuckled slightly at how we concerned ourselves with trivial knowledge instead of thinking about our current problems. "Their existance isn't tied to a physical body like you and me. If you kill their physical being, they can choose to reform or create a new one. They can also freely move around the dimensions without any physical form if they so choose."

The five youngest of us leaned forward, interested in his words. "The different dimensions?" Asher asked.

"Look, we're getting off-topic," Logan sighed.

"And you're evading the question." I pointed at him. "Is that where these soul-bonded dragons are?" The remark of real dragons he made yesterday still irked me, and so I needed to know more about these true dragons.

"One of them, yes, but there is a total of 5 living dimensions. Look, we can discuss this later. Right now, though, we need to deal with the problem that is in front of us. The coven." He emphasized the last two words to make sure we stay on topic.

"That's why I'm here," Carol interjected. "I've spent the last 18 or so years learning about them and why they are so against our family."

"Care to share? This is one of the few topics I'm not too privy to." Logan leaned back in his seat, his food having disappeared from his plate twice as fast as those around him.

"Well, for starters, the Sliver of Divinity was first founded months before World War One by a man named Smith. It's said that he was given a fraction of the god's magic. Thus, the name of the coven. This magic was taught to others across the world as they fought in the war. He set up different factions, one for each continent. In the war, they didn't fight the different nations, though. They fought dragons who were out to get their power." Logan snickered, but at Carol's glare, he let her continue without further interruption. "As the years went on, and Smith died, each faction of the coven became its own organization. The coven in North America, for example, has a completely different hierarchy system and channels to go through than South America or Asia. There is one similarity. Every faction has a representative who communicates with the other representatives."

"So why are they against our family?"

"Sliver of Divinity's goal is to eliminate dragons. Us Swallows are the biggest clan of dragons in North America and are spread out across the different countries. We've protected many smaller families who have popped up throughout the years when the coven attacks them. They believe that, by eliminating us, they could better get rid of the other families."

"Then why not attack the Windsor's when they found out they were also dragons?" The question rubbed me the wrong way. I didn't want to think about them getting hurt, but my question still stood.

Carol shrugged, speechless. "I don't know, I still haven't quite figured that out."

"Why didn't I grow up with this knowledge?" I asked, truly confused as to why I felt so out of the loop of my own family. Before two years ago, I really only had Uncle Nick. He refused to talk about family, only talking about my parents when I asked about them.

Nick cleared his throat. "Our," he gestured between himself and Aunt Carol, "mother, your grandmother died because she was helping another shifter family that was attacked by the coven. After that, I decided to move away from Arizona and come here. I needed to get away from all of the heartache that home caused. It was only a few years later that your parents were attacked and you came to live with me." I'd heard

184

that part of the story before. They were living with some distant relatives at the time and were attacked. While my parents died saving others, they left me behind, and Uncle Nick was the closest living direct relative at the time. I was only about a year old.

"I told my father and siblings I was going to be the one to raise you. That I'd keep you away from all of that. Too much of it had influenced your life already." It was only a few months after that when the Windsors moved into the park.

Asher, having finished his food, grunted to grab everyone's attention. "When Drake and I were approached by Douglas, he said something about Drake's alpha power, and that's what Lindsay was after. That could be why. Lindsay learned quickly Drake was an alpha, and then she learned about our connection to you," He gestured to me. "And then she figured she'd get two dragons with one stone." I nodded as it made sense to me. "Stay with Drake and wait around for you to return."

Henry nudged Landon's side. "Do you remember what the cunt said the other morning? When she was waiting outside the house?"

I looked over at him with a glare. "I don't like the start of this joke."

Asher smacked his forehead and groaned. Landon nodded slowly, remembering the encounter. "Yeah." Landon smiled. "Something along the lines of wanting to take our land for the coven or something."

Asher shook his head. "Not that part. It's what would be given to her if she did such a thing. She wants more power to get higher in the coven."

Landon nodded, now recalling more of the details. "I think when she was erasing and replacing Drake's memories, she was trying to figure out a way to get the alpha powers from him, too. She said something about becoming more powerful due to the process."

My glare darkened the longer my boys spoke. "The sooner we have this place warded, the better." My voice was all but a growl. "For all we know, she could pop in here at any damn time she pleases."

Nick nodded. "Carol will help us with that after breakfast, and then she and I will go car shopping. Y'all should do your rounds in the park. Stay close together to stay safe.

I knew he was right in his direction, but I didn't like how he was speaking to me. I wasn't five years old. "Doctor Logan, do you have mage problems like this where you come from?"

"Not exactly. There are several problems out there, though. Thankfully, none of you have to worry about them."

I could tell he thought our problems were minor and whatever he was dealing with, he didn't want us to find out. "Do you worry about those problems?"

"I do. That's for me to worry about, though. I have found in my many years of experience that it is best to deal with the problems you have solutions for first, rather than do nothing

and stress about bigger problems. You might just find your answer in the smaller problems."
I sat with that as the conversations around me continued. I always thought it was the big problems I needed to deal with first. Then, I wouldn't need to worry so much about the smaller problems. I'd look at the smaller problems as if they were nothing. If I can get through my bigger problems, I can get through anything.

Chapter Eleven

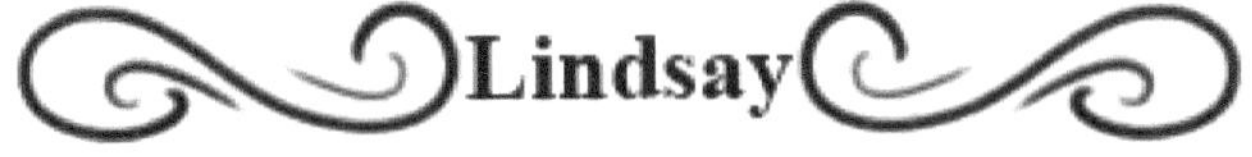

BEGRUDGINGLY, LINDSAY HAD TO ADMIT, Douglas being here had her sleeping better. Yesterday, he took them both back to his house, taking a day to focus on her studies and not worry about the mess with the alpha. Douglas, despite still sleeping in her bed, did all he could to help her.

Sitting on the floor in Douglas's study, Lindsay was surrounded by spell books. The sound of footsteps echoed in the empty hallway as the young Barlough walked closer. His humming sent soothing caresses to the back of her mind, causing her to close her eyes and focus on the song. She soon found herself humming along and swaying as she sat crisscrossed on the floor. The song was a soothing lullaby her mother used to sing to her.

When Douglas started singing words to the tune, and they weren't the correct ones, the younger mage realized what he was doing to her. Opening her eyes, Lindsay mentally shut him out. "Get out of my head, asshole. It's what we agreed on."

"How else do you plan on strengthening the use of your mind without working out those muscles?"

"I should have remembered you can't be trusted." She deadpanned, rolling her eyes when he dramatically put his hand to his chest.

"You wound me, Beautiful."

With a wave of her hand, a small glimmer of blue caused the books surrounding her on the floor to fly neatly back to their spot on the shelf. "What do you have on finding people? How do you find me so easily?"

"What you want to look into is divination." Douglas walked over to a shelf and pulled down a white book. "A common misconception about divination is that it is only about seeing the future. Seeing the future is an advanced skill." Sitting down on the floor, across from Lindsay, he leaned forward and whispered, "I do not believe even my father knows that skill yet." He leaned back and opened the book, flipping a few pages and shrugging. "Personally? I do not believe it is a true skill. If anything, it is a myth to make young mages think the high-ranking ones know what youngsters are up to when, in all reality, their parents are using divination to watch their children.

It was a trick that worked on her when she was younger. "So, how do I do it?"

"Let us go back to the basics of power. You know how to direct your mind to mine, correct?"

That was another thing Lindsay failed at. "No. I still have to touch my target."

"That is interesting." He looked her up and down, assessing how much of the basics she actually knew. "Okay, let us think of it differently." Tapping his finger on his chin, Douglas looked around and smirked, grabbing a book off the shelf. "The books, you know how to move them. Think about the feeling of your magic reaching out to the books to tell them what to do. That is your stream of power." Douglas waved his hand, and a faint blue surrounded his fingers when he commanded the book out of his hand and into Lindsay's. "It is similar to that except you need to use your power to assist in picturing your target. Think of it as calling out to your target in all directions."

Lindsay had a hard time following his logic. She could easily feel the magic coursing through her muscles as easily as she could breathe. Telling the books where to go wasn't an extension of her power as much as it was using the books' memory as to where it went and commanding them to go back. As easy as if she were talking to a person in front of her.

Seeing his line of thought was going nowhere with her, Douglas tried another train of thought. "When I tell you to picture an apple, what do you think of?" His eyes turned purple as he looked into her mind, trying to weasel into her thought process.

"You said you wouldn't." Lindsay fought the intrusion into her mind.

"I am not going to control your mind. I simply want to see what you see."

"I don't see anything! Okay?" She allowed him into her mind as he tried to walk her through visualizing different things, but, after several minutes of trying, she was no closer to being able to see through her mind's eye. Douglas was at a loss for words. "It's why it's so easy to get into and change people's minds. I don't think in pictures; I think in concepts.

Douglas thought about all the dreams he caused her to have and became even more confused. "Do you dream?"

"Not that I can remember." Lindsay shrugged. "If I put concepts into others' minds, they are the ones who form the pictures, and they are the ones who believe they came up with the thought. It's also why erasing memories or changing them comes so easily. I can't see them, so when I go through someone's memories, and I change a concept within them, they are the ones who fill in the gaps."

It took several moments for Douglas to figure out how to explain divination and teleportation without mentally visualizing the person or destination, but instead, he stood and went to the bookshelf next to the table to grab a few more books on the topic. "These might help you, and in the meantime, I will look further into this to help."

Amelia

Doing as Uncle Nick told us, we left to do our rounds of the park. Our first stop was the visitor's center to make sure all those animals were doing okay. It was Henry's favorite part of our patrols. He couldn't help but spew random facts he'd learned in his science courses to help us understand how nature worked. How he managed to keep up with his studies these past two weeks, I didn't know but was proud of him.

The trails were my favorite part. The greenery surrounding me, seeing the little things like vines hanging and secret little alcoves. The world felt alive along the trails.

With all of us staying together for safety, it took us longer to finish all of our duties, even while flying for some of it. The trails were busier than normal, and several people were welcoming me back, saying they missed me, asking me why I left, and saying how much I seemingly had grown, even though I hadn't grown an inch in the last four years.

Drake and Asher often found themselves tussling and challenging each other at every turn when there weren't people around, while the twins, Henry and Lany, walked with me as if we were on a casual stroll. The views of the water were truly breathtaking. "A penny for your thoughts?" Henry held my hand, squeezing slightly to get my attention.

"I was just thinking about all of the beauty I missed while I was away. About how selfish I want to be."

Both of the men had an eyebrow raised as they looked at me. Selfish?" Lany asked, a smirk teasing at the corner of his lips.

"I've been thinking about how comfortable you guys are with me showing P.D.A. in front of the others. Y'all never used to be so…"

"Accepting?" Henry completed my sentence.

"Yeah. I know y'all knew I was with all of you, but preferred it when it wasn't seen. Now you four actively show your affection to me in front of the others."

"Well, while you were away, and before Lindsay showed up, we all had a talk. A few, actually. We all love you and were already okay with sharing you. We agreed that, if and when we got you back, we wouldn't hold back. There is no use holding back if there is ever doubt that it might be our last time seeing you." His words sank deep.

"You don't mind sharing me, but the thought of sharing any of you with another bothers me. Am I being hypocritical? I know that if one or more of you really wanted to date someone else and fall in love, I would accept it. That was discussed when we all created this dynamic, but the thought hurts me. Is that wrong?"

"If that ever does happen, we want you to know that mythical woman would have to live up to some high standards." Lany joked before grabbing my hand and stopping, causing Henry and me to stop. Looking into his eyes, I could see the truth that whatever happens in the future, we all do it together. There was no splitting us apart again.

"I love you," I whisper before kissing him. Henry let go of my hand as Lani deepened the kiss. Pulling away, I looked at Henry and smiled, giggling before kissing him too. "I love you, too," I whispered against his lips.

"Hey! Love birds! We're done! Wanna race home?" Asher called out.

Our homes were across the lake, and with how busy it was on the trails, it wouldn't be okay to fly right now. Looking between the other three, I smiled and started running along the unmarked path to their house. "Wait, no one said go!" Lany yelled as they all started running after me. The branches sticking out tore at my jeans, so I shifted my legs enough to be covered in scales. Drake was the first to catch up to me, with Asher not too far behind.

My lungs started to burn from how hard I was running, and my legs yearned to be relieved of their duties after all the walking and running I had already accomplished during our rounds, but I pressed forward, determined not to lose. It had to be a few miles at least from our house, and there was a clearing up ahead. I could cut through to shorten the distance even more. Glancing down to jump over a log, I looked back up to see a shimmering blue line in the clearing coming up.

Both Drake and Asher cursed and grabbed me, popping out their wings to make us stop. Split seconds later, Henry and Lany ran into us, knocking all of us onto the ground. "What the actual fuck, guys?" Groaning, I slowly stood up to brush the dirt and leaves off my legs. "What was that for?" I glared at them before looking back up to see what the shimmering light was. It wouldn't have been the first time the light had played tricks on my eyes, nor the first time I've hallucinated. I watched as Lindsay stepped out of the shimmering line, and rage began to boil in my chest. "I'm going to kill her." Rage burned in my eyes. Drake grabbed my arm when he stood, causing me to whip my head back to look at him. Fear and adrenaline pumped through my veins at the thought that he was once again under her spells. Seeing the anger and concern in his eyes, I could tell he wasn't, but why would he stop me? This was my chance!

A flash of shock on her face was covered up quickly with her smile. "Well, lookie who it is," Lindsay sing-songed. "I do wish that you'd take care of yourself a bit more so you're not so dirty, Drakey. It doesn't look good on you." A growl ripped through my chest, causing Drake's grip on my arm to tighten. My fingers were already shifted to claws, and as I clenched my fist, they dug into the palms of my hands, causing me to bleed. The pain didn't even cross my mind while all of my focus was on the mage walking towards us. With every step she took, the need to claw her eyes out grew.

"Leave." My voice was strained as I held back everything in warning. "Now." It would be the only warning she would get.

"We aren't even on your property. You can't tell me what to do." The giggle that came from her lips and the casual "oh well" shrug of her shoulders had me pulling away from Drake. Asher quickly pulled me back, allowing Drake to get a better hold.

Unable to form coherent words any longer, my mouth opened and closed with no sound. Instead, small droplets of my neon green acid breath slowly ran down my chin. Lany spoke up. "How would you know if we were or not? I doubt you know where her estate starts and stops." Lany stepped forward, getting between Lindsay and me, and though I could tell he was trying to do so in a way to calm me down, it did anything but.

"Funny thing about that." I will rip that smug smile right off her face. She will be begging for mercy, of which I have none. "My father has tried, time and time again, to get on her family's land for the past two years. It was the weirdest thing, though. Every time he tried, he couldn't set foot on your land without all his magic and strength being drained." She used her fingers for emphasis as she counted different objects. "Stones, books, wands, even cards didn't help him. All of their magic leaves the object after passing the threshold." She took another step towards her death at my hands, her arms outstretched to her sides, just asking for me to throw the first punch.

"Your kind of magic isn't welcome on *our* land." I tried to move closer, but the hold my boys had on me didn't budge, instead, tightening around my arms. I knew I'd have bruises on my arms after this, and it would be all my own doing. My boys wouldn't be holding me back like this if I could control myself, but this absolute cunt of a leech wouldn't get out of this alive if I had any say in the matter.

Ignoring my hostility, Lindsay took yet another step closer. "And wouldn't you have it, we just tried to teleport into the Windsor's manor just now and couldn't? Just like my father couldn't teleport into your land." There was something off with her words. Who was this "we" she was talking about? If there were several of them, where were they? Why was she alone now? She had to be lying.

Henry stepped forward so he stood next to Lany. "It's just as Amelia said, in case you didn't hear, your magic isn't welcome on *our* land."

Deep breath in. Deep breath out. I did my best to breathe, to calm down, but they came out as growls, fueling my rage instead. Between Henry and Landon, I watched Lindsay blink a few times, realizing what he meant. Huffing, she put her hands on her hips. "It won't be your land for long." She glared at us but didn't dare lock eyes with me.

"That's it!" I shifted enough to grow and cause the grip of the two Windsors who were holding me to loosen. Pushing away from them and through the other two, I sprinted towards the mage. Adrenaline let me ignore my previous aches and pains of mere minutes ago. A sudden gust of wind hit my side just before I was within arm's reach, pushing me to the right.

"What's wrong?" Lindsay blinked a few times as her smile grew. "Come on." I hated the cocky grin on her face as she leaned forward. "Hit me." Never one to back down, I ran at her again, ready for the wind blast this time. This time, the wind hit me harder, blasting around her, creating her own personal tornado. She couldn't do this forever. I might not know much about her magic, but I knew she couldn't breathe inside that cyclone. All I needed to do was stay in it until she suffocated herself.

Standing within the area of wind was hard enough. Throwing a punch was almost impossible, and it wouldn't have the impact I wanted. Locking eyes with her, I could see she would go longer than I could stay in the wind's onslaught, so I took a step back to reassess the situation. "Can't do it? I knew you were weak."

Thick neon green liquid started oozing from the corners of my mouth, dripping onto the leaves below. The small sizzling sound could be heard as it started to disintegrate the leaves. The taste of my acid was sweet, almost like sour candy, but it was deadly. Watching to see what she might do next, I held back the acid, letting it build, and could feel my throat shifting to hold it.

Lindsay muttered something under her breath, and her fingertips started to glow purple, but I wasn't going to chance anything. Letting the acid in my throat out, I let loose a torrent of acid at the mage. The purple quickly faded from her fingertips to be replaced with orange as Lindsay conjured an orange shield of runes in the air. Keeping at it for as long as I could, I watched my acid eat away at the edges of her shield. The smell of deteriorating magic was not what I would have expected, as the air heated with steam. I stopped, needing to breathe in, and smirked at the horrified look on her face. "There's more where that came from." I bluffed. While I could spit out a tad bit more, I couldn't breathe it out like that again until I could build enough back up in my throat. To prove my point, though, I spat the excess from the back of my throat at her feet.

The brunette mage looked between me and the ground dissolving at her feet, and I fed off the fear in her eyes. I didn't care about the wind contingency she seemed to have. I was not going to let her get her manipulative hands on Drake, or any of my boys, again. Going forward, the wind no longer circulated in one direction; instead, it whipped around us chaotically. Both of our hair whipped around us, but I pushed through, reaching out with my claws to tear her apart. IN a mirror action, I swiped my claw, and she waved her hand. My claw missed; her magic having thrown me to the side, my head slamming against a tree. I could feel the warmth of blood trickle down the back of my head.

The sounds of a car crash echoed in my mind. Holding the sides of my head, I blinked, and the world around me blurred.

~~~ ~~~ ~~~

The nervousness I felt, my stomach twisted with excitement. "What do you hope it will be?" My Aunt Carol asked, glancing over at me. Smiling softly, I looked down at my slightly swollen abdomen. "Boy or girl?"

I think to myself, picturing a sweet baby girl, with a red bow in her blonde hair that she got from Drake or Henry, or a white bow in her red hair she inherited from Lany or Asher. Looking up at me with my own brown eyes. With either
~~~

golden flakes donated by Drake or Lany, or shimmering blue in the light from Henry or Asher. I didn't say anything out loud, though, just praying I had a healthy baby. "As long as they are healthy, I'll be happy and, maybe one day, they might get to meet their daddy."

"Have you at least thought about names?"

"If she's a girl, her name would be either Seraph or Mary. If he's a boy, Azriel or maybe Gabriel."

"Those are beautiful names. I can't wait to hold little Azriel." I turned up the music, singing along to one of my favorite songs.

"Amelia!" My aunt's voice cried out. Flashes of red and brown around me. There was the sound of times squealing before pain in the back of my head, the side of my head. Shit. My leg screamed in searing pain. A roar came from my aunt as she shifted into a dragon, and the car around me moved. We were on the edge of a mountain road, and with her shift, the car fell, tumbling down the mountain, only stopping when it hit the road beneath us. I was upside down, only being held by the seatbelt. I needed to get out. I wasn't safe. I knew I was fading in and out, not being able to tell if it was seconds, minutes, or hours between closing and opening my eyes. Reaching for the seatbelt buckle, I clicked it, immediately regretting it when I fell, hitting my head again. Fuck! My hand went to my abdomen. "It's okay. Momma will protect you.

I needed to shift, but my leg was in so much pain. The act of shifting would feel as if I were tearing it apart. No, I had to get out of the car first. Easy enough, the windows around me were all broken during the fall. It was getting harder to breathe, and blood covered my hands. Whether it was blood from my head or if I cut myself with the glass under me, I couldn't tell. Everything hurt. There were sounds of explosions above me and rocks falling onto the car. The screeching of tires echoing in my ears. Why did everything have to be so loud?

"Ma'am?" A male voice called out. I don't know him. Can I trust him? "Ma'am! Are you okay?" He asks, and I close my eyes. My body. I need to assess my body. What hurts? What doesn't hurt? My hand reached for my abdomen, praying my baby was okay. "Can you hear me?" I groan in an answer. "I'm going to pull you out!" I feel hands around my arms, and I scream in pain as my leg is jostled. As I held onto my abdomen with one hand, I couldn't feel my opposite arm. So much pain. This is it. I'm dying." Tears roll down my cheek. I'm not good enough, not strong enough to keep us alive.

"Fuck!" I hear him yell as more explosions above us cause rocks to fall onto us, making it harder to breathe with dust clouding in the air around us. "Can you wal-" His question cut short as he saw what state of being I was in. "I'm going to call an ambulance!" He pulled out his phone and quickly dialed 911. "Holy Fuck." He spoke in awe as I heard the dispatch operator on the other line. Looking up, I saw my aunt, a full dragon, flying into the sky and letting out her lightning breath. "Is… is that a dragon?" The man trying to save me took a few steps back in disbelief, maybe fear.

"She's nice. My… Aunt." Words were hard. He looked down at me as if I were crazy.

The woman on the other end of his phone said she had located where he was via his phone and was sending out an officer to see what was going on. It was then that he got his wits about him again, bringing the phone to his ear once more. "Ambulance, there was a car crash from up the mountain. I need an ambulance. There is a pregnant woman who needs medical attention."

One more lightning blast from above sent a volley of rocks our way. The world went black again.

Drake

Once Amelia hit the tree, the four Windsors bolted, Landon and Asher to Lindsay, while Drake and Henry went to Amelia, who shifted into her dragon form, roaring in pain. Drake's hands immediately went to Amelia's head, his words empowered with his alpha presence. "Amelia, baby. Come back to me." He could see, with how out of focus her eyes were, that she was not there currently. "You're okay." It wasn't necessarily the truth, but it was what she needed to hear.

Henry quickly went to work patching up her head, helped by the enhanced healing they had in their dragon form. He pet her wings, putting himself between her and the tree she kept hitting her head against.

"Baby," Drake whispered. "Concentrate on the heat." He blew warm air on her snout. "Look around. Try to name five things you can see." He took a deep breath before another, doing his best to try to get her to mimic his breathing. "Five things you can see, four things you can touch." She wasn't hearing him, and so he put more force into his words. "Amelia." Drake never begged for anything, but he'd beg for her to come back to him any, and every day he'd be allowed to breathe if it meant she'd be okay. "Count with me." He looked into her glazed-over eyes. "One: Trees with thick branches that go sky high. Two: The ground covered with sicks and dying leaves. Three: a cloudy blue and white sky." Deep breath in, deep breath out. "Four: Your four boys who love you and need you here with us." He could see her blink a few times, eyes wildly looking around. "Five, the beautiful blue water crashing against the Cypress knees."

"She's not bleeding anymore," Henry informed his brother, who looked up at him and nodded. "Now, four things you can feel." Drake looked at his other two brothers fighting the mage, doing their best not to cause a forest fire, spitting small blasts of fire to catch her off guard before attempting to strike at her. "Go help them." He ordered Henry, who nodded and jumped over the black dragon, who stopped moving. "Three things you can hear." Another exaggerated deep breath and exhale, breathing warm air against her. "Two things you can smell. One thing you can taste." His inner dragon yearned to soothe the hurting woman, yet she still cried out, closing her eyes and loudly roaring out in pain, swishing her tail violently.

Amelia

Beep… Beep… Beep…

It smelled sterile, and as I tried to move, I felt awful. I couldn't move most of me, and the other half was numb

Beep… Beep… Beep…

Where was I? The lights were too bright as I tried to open my eyes.

Beep… Beep… Beep…

It finally registered what that sound was, and sorrow filled my entire being. I knew what that wound was. It was one heartbeat. My heartbeat.

Beep… Beep… Beep…

"Amelia." Drake's voice echoed in my mind, causing tears to fall faster. What will he think of me? I wasn't good enough. I couldn't keep it. "Amelia, baby." His soothing voice felt like a hug. "You're okay." His words were lies. I was anything but okay. Drake didn't know. Henry, Landon, and Asher didn't know. My uninjured arm went to my bandaged abdomen. I lost them, all of them.

 Asher

Lindsay prepared for the attacks from the now three dragons, casting shield spell after shield spell, doing her best to land an attack on at least one of the dragons in between.

Asher was grateful Lindsay's wind defense went away after Amelia was thrown into a tree, but he had to admit, Amelia crying out in pain was a huge distraction for both himself and Landon. They could only trust that their older brothers were on it, helping her in ways they couldn't. Unlike Amelia, he knew their goal wasn't Lindsay's death. Their goal was to subdue. Unfortunately, that goal was hard if they couldn't touch her. Landon started spitting small fire blasts at her as a distraction while Asher took swipes at her.

When Henry joined in, it got easier, but with one punch from Landon, Lindsay grabbed his arm, and purple magic strands wove themselves around his arm. Time seemed to slow as the purple strands wrapped around Landon's neck. The mental connection she felt with Landon was gone as quickly as it came.

Asher sent a well-timed kick to her side, causing her to lose her grip on his brother. *"New goal. Subdue the mage without letting her touch any of them. Easy,"* Asher sarcastically thought to himself.

Amelia

I lay on my bed in my grandfather's house, the day after my casts were taken off. I felt hollow, with no goals, no feeling inside me. The doctors were wrong. I wasn't fully healed, and I strongly doubted I ever would be. I wouldn't be recovered until those bastards who took my child were dead by my hand. Physically, I might be fine. Mentally, I had a lot of work to do.

I stood up, rubbing my new scar with newly found determination. "Please, come back to me, Baby." Drake's voice stopped me from moving. "Breathe with me. In… Out." The feeling of his warm air surrounded me. "What are five things you can see?" His soft voice grounded me, and I blinked, trying to focus on anything. "Four things you can feel." I moved my hands around and felt the ground. Blinking a few times, my surroundings changed, and I felt my tail rubbing the forest floor. "Three things you can hear." He started to hum a soft melody I couldn't help but hum along to. "Good girl." He kissed my snout. "Okay, Baby, what are two things you can smell?"

Burning. Something is on fire. Not the smell of car smoke. A campfire, perhaps? The scent of Drake was strong, the smell of fresh grilled meat and potatoes.

"What can you taste? One thing."

I still had that sweetly sour taste of my acid. I could hear the breath of relief Drake let out when I looked around, dizzy.

What was happening? My boys were losing their fight. Lindsay grabbed Asher as the youngest Windsor went for a punch, and she could see the purple glow of her fingertips. "Asher!" I mentally cried out and realized I needed to shift back into my human form. Drake glanced back at the fight and, seeing two of his brothers on the ground, growled, gaining the attention of Lindsay.

"Fucking Hells." She glared at me. "Put some fucking clothes on!" It wasn't just her voice saying those words. Asher's unwilling voice spoke in time with Lindsay's. She then grabbed Henry's arm as he groaned, trying to roll away from her. After a subtle glow from her fingertips, she let go of both the Windsor boys and put her hands to her forehead. "Damn it!"

I, unable to move most of my body, sat with my back against the tree and watched Drake walk up to the mage. All four Windsors stood around Lindsay as the mage struggled with something, rocking back and forth with her palms against her head. "You have no business being here." Drake spat as he walked in front of the mage. On the side of the alpha's neck were slits glowing red, and flames fell out of his mouth like lava while he spoke. "You've not only done damage to me, but your coven has done more damage to our mate than can be repented for." Even from the side angle I had, I could see the fear of life in Lindsay's eyes. The mage finally realized she'd flown too close to the sun.

Lindsay took a glance at me, and I froze as if she transferred that fear into me. Is she the one who caused me to have those flashbacks? Was it her playing mind games? I haven't had flashbacks that bad for the past year, since I was allowed to get off my meds. My nightmares hadn't even been that bad.

Watching her mouth inaudible words, I felt more than saw a thin red line on the ground getting closer to me. The smile on her lips was the last thing I felt before the line around me constricted against me, causing hot, searing pain. The pain traveled from my skin to cramping my muscles to bone-deep pain. My screech caused the four Windsor boys to look at me. "Drake!" Henry rushed to me, and his feet on the ground were the last thing I registered before everything went white.

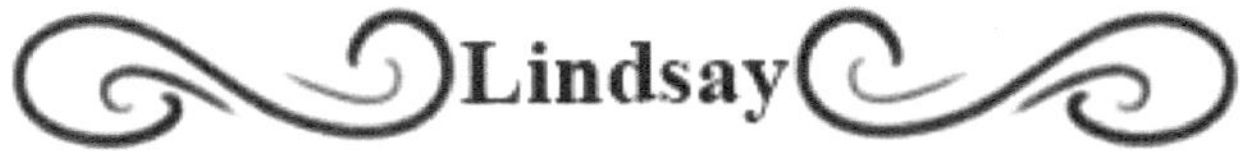

Lindsay

Lindsay smiled, knowing it was only a matter of time before the female shifter was no more. When she looked back at Drake, who was distracted, she grabbed his leg and attempted to reconnect to his inner mind.

Opening her eyes, she saw Douglas yanking her to her feet, having teleported them a few yards away from the circled Windsor men. "Let go of me!" She yelled, causing the confused shifters to look in her direction. Pushing away from the other mage, Lindsay yelled and brushed the dirt off herself. "Go away! I can take care of this myself!" Electricity danced across her fingers before she directed the pure energy away from her, in the direction of Douglas. Disappointment grew as Douglas swatted his hand, redirecting the electricity towards the screaming dragon shifter on the ground.

"Do not be stupid, my love. You were about to be executed by incineration." His calm words irritated her more, but at this point, any words he spoke that weren't "I will leave you to it" would anger her.

"I have it all under control." She insisted, seeing Drake's glare bounce between her and the overdressed male.

Douglas put a hand out, causing Drake to flip and land on his back, the alpha shifter letting out a groan. "You obviously needed my help. Now, come with me."

"No!" Lindsay shot several more lightning bolts of her energy at Douglas before her energy felt drained. The man took advantage of her weakened state and grabbed her arm, pulling her. "I can still hold my own. I almost had her!" She shouted, taking a glance at the naked woman who was still yelling in pain on her back, paralyzed. The image faded once Lindsay was pulled through a portal to the front door of her family's bakery.

Chapter Twelve

LINDSAY FOUGHT BOTH PHYSICALLY AND mentally as Douglas pulled her up the stairs to her home above the bakery, the window showing her ditz of a mother placing another dozen cupcakes into the oven to bake. "Let me go back!"

"How did you even get there?" Douglas grunted as he tugged her along, "I leave for five minutes and come back with some news when you went off and got yourself in a deadly, one-on-five match against dragons." He opened the door leading to her living room, but Lindsay finally loosened his grip enough to slip out of it before he could pull her through. He quickly recovered by grabbing her jacket sleeve and yanking her through the door, causing her to fall onto the floor.

"You absolute asshole!" Slapping his hands away from her when he reached out to help her stand, Lindsay simply gave him a glare that could kill as she stood on her own. Getting back there wouldn't be easy, hells, getting there in the first place was hard enough. Now, without the assistance of the runes and sigil book, she wouldn't be able to try again. Slamming the door, she turned back around to Douglas. "I was doing just fine on my own! She would have been dead by now!"

"And you might have been, too! Tell me, do you have good enough shields to block their fire? The lava from all four of them?"

Too angry to admit he might be right, she kept yelling. "She might be dead right now, but I wouldn't know, now, would I? Fuck! You could have even helped by attacking the others, but no, you had to get me out of there as fast as possible!" Looking into Douglas's eyes, she could see them flash purple before she closed out any thoughts other than her own. "No! You won't be changing my mind!" She fought for a few minutes as he dug further into her soul. Lindsay wouldn't let him control her decisions. He needed to take her back to the dead or dying bitch to make sure she's finished off.

"Lindsay?" The voice of her father caused her to open her eyes and stand straighter. Both Alvin and Amber ran into the room. The look in her father's eyes told her she was inconveniencing him.

The young mage in question lowered her head. "I'm sorry. Douglas just," She dared take a glance towards the black-haired man, "interrupted while I was trying to finish off a Swallow."

Douglas scoffed. "You were about to be burned alive by all four of the male dragons." He leaned over her, trapping her with his arm on the wall next to her.. "And like you said, she could very well be dead right now. I simply didn't want your death."

"I was this close," She held up her pointer finger and thumb millimeters apart to emphasize her point, "to commanding Drake again, and his brother Landon wasn't too far behind either.

"You still need to touch them in order to get into their minds." Douglas scoffed. "There was no way you would have gotten out of there scot-free if I had not shown up."

Amber's gaze softened, and she put a hand on Alvin's arm. "Lindsay, I am sure he only went to you because you were in danger. Taking on five dragons is ambitious for someone of your rank." Lindsay wouldn't be talked down to like this. Stomping up the stairs, she headed to her room to try and replicate what she did to teleport the first time.

"Lindsay," Douglas spoke from the other side of her closed door.

"Fuck off, Douglas!" She yelled behind her, sitting at her desk.

Instead of doing what she desired most, the man walked in and closed the door behind him with a barely audible click, silently sitting on her bed. "My stepmother is right."

"I told you," Tears filled with anger threatened to fall, "to fuck off." The calm in her whispered voice spoke volumes about how close she was to the edge. So sick and tired of being told she wasn't powerful enough. It wasn't her fault that everyone kept limiting her to this box. If only she were given a chance, or enough resources to learn the more advanced magics, she could prove herself worthy.

"I get it." He leaned forward with his elbows on his knees. "You would rather not hear it. Let me help you. Come back with me. Leave someone else to take care of those dragons." This wasn't the first time he'd asked her to come back to his place and live with him, to get away from her father. The issue always being: it wouldn't get her away from her father. It would just be another excuse for her father and Douglas's stepmother to spend more time together, and Lindsay's mother didn't deserve that. The offer was always tempting, but it also always came with give and take. He would provide her with resources, and in turn, she would need to be willing to have a romantic relationship with him. He was insufferable at the best of times. The sound of a romantic relationship with him put a bad taste in her mouth.

Lindsay realized she'd been silent too long with him staring at her, waiting for an answer. "I'll agree to come over again today."

"And have dinner?" There it was, the strings attached.

"What are you cooking?" It was a trick question. They both knew he hardly knew how to boil water. The man had servants to do everything for him, allowing him to spend all his time on studies.

Douglas chuckled. "If I'm cooking, you should have a fire extinguisher handy." He leaned back, now half lying on the bed with his hands under his head. "What would you like?"

"To eat alone." She mumbled to herself before speaking clearly. "Surprise me. I'm sure anything your cook makes will be fantastic."

"Deal." Douglas smiled. "Did you want to pack a bag or bring anything?"

"If I need anything from this room, you'll bring me back without question." The stare she gave him showed there was no fighting her on that fact. The raven-haired man nodded in agreement and put his arm out for her to take. With a deep breath, she took it, and he led her back out of her room to the living room.

"Lindsay." Amber smiled from the kitchen, where Al was brooding. "I just got word from my husband." She bounced over and placed a hand on her shoulder, Lindsay doing her best not to shrug her off. "He would like to have a meeting with you." At the mention of a meeting with George Bar-lough, Lindsay paused. This could be the meeting she was waiting for. If he offered her more than Douglas, without any romantic strings attached, Lindsay would leap at the chance.

A hand snaking around her waist made her jump slightly, and she narrowed her eyes at Douglas. "Don't touch me. I'm still mad at you."

Douglas took his hand off her and nodded. "As you wish, my sweet, but my father isn't someone who likes to wait; you've only managed to teleport once, and you don't know the sigil for the house." He winked. "If you wish to join us in the meeting, you need to sort through your anger rather quickly." He smugly walked over to the blank wall.

Alvin and Amber both smiled at Lindsay as she put her annoyance in check. Her fingers sparked with small bolts of electricity jumping from finger to finger. If she weren't so sure Douglas would counter her magic, she would have cursed him a long time ago. Taking a deep breath to calm herself, the young mage watched as Douglas finished drawing the transportation sigil on the wall. She knew it was useless to try and memorize the runes due to the fact that, if she messed it up even slightly, she'd be transported somewhere else. Lindsay, holding Douglas's hand, and the two older adults' hand on their shoulder, walked through the baby blue portal that formed.

She found herself at the front driveway of the Barlough Mansion. Douglas opened the double doors and gestured for her to walk in before him, giving a slight bow. Rolling her eyes, she walked in and up the spiral staircase to the right. Lindsay had only been to George's office a couple of times, but one thing that stood out was that he wanted his office to

216

be on the top floor, giving the feeling of looking out on his kingdom.

The closed door to his office caused her to stop and step to the side. Only a few people could simply walk into George's office without consequence, and his wife, Amber, was one of them. The blonde waltzed into the room with a smile on her face, as if she wasn't cheating on the man mere minutes ago. Douglas grabbed her hand, guiding her into the room next, and her father closed the door behind them.

The walls were covered in bookshelves with windows between them, the books being several old potion and spell books. With a glance, she saw a whole shelf dedicated to transportation runes.

Runes and sigils would be her best route to figuring out Transportation. Lindsay wouldn't need to picture where she was going if she used the right sigils to take her places. She'd done it once, and with enough time and understanding, she could do it again.

George sat behind his desk with his hands folded under his chin. The man was a spitting image of Douglas, the major differences being George's features were more aged, and the older man's recently shaven, maybe even waxed, head. "Lindsay, it's lovely to see you again." The older mage stood. "Douglas has told me much of your past two years." Lindsay turned to glare suspiciously at Douglas. "And your... dealings with the shifters there."

Doing her best to keep her composure, the young female smiled sweetly. "He has, has he?"

"Yes. I'm glad to see you alive, as well. He left in a hurry, saying you were in a skirmish with them?" Although he stated it as a question, he didn't leave room for her to give an answer. "What I don't like to hear is that someone in my coven has not only not disclosed the location of a new family of dragons but has also gotten so close to them." The tone coming from George hinted at how he also didn't like hearing that his son's chosen female was getting romantically attached to a dragon.

"It's not like that!" She tried to defend herself. There was no way Douglas's jealousy would get between her and a higher ranking of magic. "I've been trying to find out where the Swallows went. Then, I was trying to gain land and power from the Windsors. I wasn't," She took a breath, "I *am* not attached to them. I was in the middle of offing Amelia Swallow when *your son* decided I wasn't able to defend myself and pulled me out of there. Unwillingly, I might add."

"If he thought you were not fit to finish the fight, it sounds like you are not mindful enough of your own limitations. That you are not ready to have the responsibility of more power."

George was about to continue with his displeased speech when the soft hum of a portal opened, and the tapestry hanging on the wall behind him moved to the side. A large, bald man with several slash scars across his face walked through. Pitch-black angel wings that matched his black-on-black suit fluttered slightly on his back. The man's golden, piercing eyes met Lindsay's before landing on George. "Update," was all he said, his voice calm and collected, but demanding and urgent

218

all the same. Power radiated from the angel, and Lindsay felt even weaker in his presence, almost undeserving of being around him. He was likely only in his mid-40s, but his eyes had such depth to them, showing he'd seen and been through more than the average 40 years.

Lindsay's eyes widened, watching the proud leader of the coven she knew shrink back in his seat. "I… um… yes. Well, I don't have much." George scrambled to find important papers on his desk that were neatly sorted before his panicked shuffling.

"I don't have time for your nonsense, *human*," He spat out that last word as if disgusted to speak it, "Do you, or do you not have updates on the dragon shifters?" The tall man placed a heavy hand on the desk. The thud silenced everyone in the room, and even the paper shuffling stopped.

Seeing this as an opportunity of a lifetime, Lindsay raised a hand slightly. "I have updates, Sir." At least, she hoped she had the updates the angel wanted.

The angelic man looked at her and then at the others in the room. When his eyes met hers again, he spoke. "Leave." Shivers of fear went up her back as she quickly turned to leave, but when her hand touched the doorknob, the angel spoke again. "Except, you two." When she turned around, she saw him pointing to George as well as herself. Douglas was rendered speechless, and once Lindsay stepped away from the door, Douglas, Amber, and Alvin all rushed out of the room.

"I'm sorry. Please forgive my outburst." She put her head down, for fear of retaliation, but suddenly felt compelled to look up and tell the man her life story.

"You said you have an update. Let's hear it." The angel crossed his arms impatiently.

Swallowing the lump in her throat, Lindsay took a deep breath. "I've spent the last two years getting to know the problem and solving it in Tennessee." At her words, the angel took a glaring glance towards George. "I attempted to get rid of one of the Swallow clan when I was rudely interrupted by Douglas for this meeting." She took this opportunity to mimic the angel's actions and glare at the man she was trying to suck up to, not two minutes ago. With all of the power emanating from the tall, bald man, she could feel that the angel had so much more to offer her than George ever could. "I can also tell you even more about the Windsors."

The angel's annoyance grew the longer she spoke, causing fear to bubble in her stomach. At her last words, the angel's fist glowed black, forcing George to be lifted from his seat. "Who are the Windsors?" The angel spoke between gritted teeth. "And why haven't I heard of them before?"

In a panicked voice, George spoke. "I only just found out about them!"

The angel looked at him suspiciously before checking with Lindsay. "How long have you been dealing with these Windsors?"

This was it. The moment that would change her life; the moment she would have the upper hand on George, and if she didn't take it now, she'd regret it for the rest of her life. Never again would she be forced to interact with Douglas, and she would possibly have more power than the leader of her coven. "Two years. I was sent to deal with the two Swallows who lived in Tennessee at the time, but they had suddenly disappeared from our radar. That's when I found the Windsors." She didn't dare say more, fearing it would give her whole hand away before she could negotiate for more power.

The angel dropped the mage back in the chair. "So, you're telling me, you assigned this *girl* to take care of one of the biggest thorns in my side, and she's been taking care of other shifters while you've been trying to find any trace of them?!" The angel took a deep breath, his voice turning oddly calm, which only made his words scarier. "And you didn't even know about it?"

As if finally gaining his backbone, George stood up. "Smoke, I sent her father after the Swallows. I would never send a child off to do something so important. After they weren't able to be found, I ordered his family to stay while others searched for them in case they showed up again. She was just a low-powered mage when I sent her father. She's still not all that powerful. My son went and saved her ass before she got herself killed."

Ignoring the latter part of what was said, Smoke turned to Lindsay. "What has your father been doing for the past two years?"

Lindsay almost burst out laughing. Her father was comfortable in the position he was in. A wife to do everything and a mistress to fuck when he desired. Hells, the bakery was even run by her mother and herself. "Watches the days go by, and when he gets bored, my father calls George's wife up for a fun time." She knew she dropped a bombshell as George hadn't known about his wife's infidelity until now. "My father doesn't have a right to the power he's gotten from his rank. I've been the one who has been trying to gain power by manipulating the Windsors."

Smoke nodded, accepting what had happened and that he now needed to keep a better eye on this sector of the coven. "What was your name, human?"

"Lindsay." The brunette smiled.

"Age?" His eyebrow rose, looking her up and down as if to say she still might be too young.

"22, Sir."

He shook his head, causing Lindsay's heart to drop. "I don't have the time for this." He sighed and then looked between the two humans in the room. "Lindsay, you've caught my interest. It's a dangerous place to find yourself because now you have to either keep it or die trying." She couldn't tell if his words were a threat or a promise. His finger traced the sigil on the wall behind the tapestry, and it started to glow. "I'll send you to my office. Wait for me there and don't touch anything. I'll be there in a short while. I still have some words for George over here." The angel finished his sentence as he finished tracing the sigil. A portal opened, and he stepped to the side. "While you're waiting, make sure you try to remember everything you know about both the Swallows and the Windsors."

Lindsay nodded and hurried, stepping through the portal and into a room with black, wooden panels covering the walls. The room was practically empty, with only a golden desk and black chair inside. There were two doors, one behind the desk and one behind where she stood, in front of the desk. Everything had ornate golden carvings on it, and while she could recognize some of them as specific runes, others were too foreign to her. Taking a second to breathe, she realized what she'd just done and knew there was no going back now.

Walking around the room, making sure to do as she was told and not touch anything, Lindsay admired the designs on the desk. The only thing she knew the meaning of in the etched golden carvings covering the desk was what looked to be a nameplate on the edge closest to her, reading "Smoke Gold" and the words under it reading, "King's Champion". With the sound of a portal, she turned around to see the tall man walk through and scowl down at her.

"We have things to do, but first, report." He sat down in his chair, casually, and she took a deep breath, doing her best to recall the last two years.

Chapter Thirteen

COLD. MORE THAN COLD, FREEZING. ECHOES of something in the distance. Voices? Maybe. Everything hurt, but in a numb way, in a way in which my limbs felt heavy and swollen

Wet. Fuck, why couldn't I open my eyes? Was I in water? Groans of pain leave my lips as I put all my effort into moving my freezing arms.

Ice. Water softly swished when I was slowly able to shift my arm in painful movements, but I could also feel the ice bump against my body. All I could think of was a glass of ice water being swirled around to make the water cooler faster.

Think. What was the last thing I could remember? I was in the woods. Drake and Henry were holding and soothing me. It came as a flash in my mind what happened, the blinding pain I was in, but it still left me confused as to how I'd gotten into my current situation.

With more effort than I'd like to admit, my eyes slowly adjusted as I opened my heavy lids to see the ceiling of my bathroom in the Windsor Manor. How in the Hells did I get here? Looking down at myself, I could see my limbs wrapped in a green cloth, and I was, indeed, submerged in an ice bath. A comforting hand reached out and lightly held my own that peeked out of the water. "You're awake," Henry whispered, relief pouring off him.

"How long was I out?" I almost didn't recognize my voice when I spoke. The rasp ached in my chest with every word spoken.

"Only a few minutes, thanks to the Doc." Henry smiled and leaned over, kissing my lips softly before pulling away as if I were a dandelion he'd blow the seeds off of. "We're lucky Doctor Chester was still here when we arrived. He said the magic used on you was something he'd only seen a handful of times. It only affected your muscles with no outward signs of damage." Henry spoke in awe as he talked about everything Doctor Chester did, including the green slime that was put onto the bandages before he helped the doctor wrap my arms and legs. "He said we were lucky it stopped when it did because it would have disintegrated your bones had it gone for just a few more minutes.

"Did anyone else get hurt?" The pain my body felt minuscule compared to the thought of anyone else getting hurt, or worse.

"Not really. Doctor Chester gave a few pills to Landon and Drake because the cunt got into their heads. Thankfully, she didn't get in far enough to change anything, but their heads hurt for a while." I growled, ready for another fight against her, and tried to get up before Henry put a hand on my shoulder to stop me. "Hey, it's okay. They are okay. You know, that anger of yours is going to get you into some serious trouble one day. You should always take a second to evaluate your surroundings and think before acting on your emotions." His words were so familiar, I would swear Henry just finished talking with my uncle Nick.

"I know." I sighed. "It wouldn't be the first time." I mentally thanked my aunt before smiling at my man. "Can I get up, though? This ice is starting to get to me."

Henry smiled and picked me up, taking me to the bed in my room. "I'll go get the doc to assess you before you're allowed to get up."

I watched his bare, muscular back as he walked out, closing the door behind him. Fuck, I could never tire of seeing my men shirtless. The yelling from downstairs stopped soon after Henry left, and several heavy footsteps ran up the stairs. My boys pushed each other to be first in the room, and stopped at my bedside, asking if I was okay, how I felt, saying how they were so glad everything worked so quickly. Doctor Chester walked in, carrying a white briefcase with several red markings, and placed it on the side table. "Alright, boys, I need you to move out of the way." They did as they were told, and Henry walked in, carrying another white briefcase with similar red markings. Doctor Logan began taking off my bandages and assessing any damages before opening the case to reveal several syringes and pouches of green liquid. Despite the green liquid, the pouches were labeled black. "How are you feeling, kiddo?"

That was a loaded question, and I didn't even know where to begin, but the doc probably meant physically. "I feel okay. Nothing hurts anymore, if that's what you're asking."

"Is it?" Wasn't that what he was asking? With the bandages removed from my right arm, he took out a syringe and filled it, using the green pouches. The color reminded me of the acid I can spit.

"Is it not what you're asking?"

"I'm more than just a doctor to take care of your physical health. Mental health is important too. I asked, 'How are you feeling?' Would you like to answer differently?"

Deciding it was best to air out my dirty laundry, I groaned. "I feel… out of control." Even saying that, it felt like an understatement. "I can't fight without being taken out with a hit to the head." I moved the arm he wasn't poking and prodding to the back of my head, where I felt a slight bump. Though I was moving slowly, as if moving through sludge, it didn't hurt.

Dr. Logan shrugged. "If it weren't for these four, you'd be dead. Any much longer in the death circle, you wouldn't have made it. They got you here quickly, and I hadn't left here since breakfast. I've been carrying around a suitcase in my truck for both your draconic color as well as theirs since I found out what color dragon you and your uncle were." I looked at the four other men in the room, my men.

"I'm just so angry. No. I'm pissed off at that damned coven. They've done nothing but ruin my life." Asher squeezed my leg, reassuringly. "They took everything from me and still weren't satisfied." A lump grew in my throat, doing my best to hold back tears. I wasn't going to cry about it again until the coven was destroyed.

"We'll get them," Drake reassured me. "I've been trying to convince Nick and Carol to let us go after them. Doc, over here, says you should be good as golden once you get a pack or two inside of you."

"Do we even know where they are?" Hope sparked in my chest. Hope that I'd be able to take my revenge on the mages.

Dr. Chester cleared his throat. "As much as I think you should wait, you will be okay in a minute, and I do have the ability to locate them."

"You didn't think of mentioning that downstairs?" Drake spoke between his teeth, obviously annoyed that the doctor didn't speak up during the conversation to back him up.

The doctor chuckled. "You have much to learn. As intimidating as you believe you are, you have yet to see what a feral dragon is capable of. However, I do believe, if you give this coven too much time, they will create a force that is too strong to be taken down by just the five of you." The doctor looked down at his side at the floor, lovingly. "It looks like the family bakery has a little secret."

We all looked at the man as if he were crazy when he started to pet the air. "Doc?" Landon asked.

"Oh, I should probably introduce him." Dr. Chester smiled and took off a collar from the invisible creature, allowing it to be seen. "This is Okin. My soul bond." The small dragon nodded towards all of us, as if to say hello.

"Holy crap." The grey dragon wasn't much bigger than a house cat. I hadn't seen a dragon that small since we were children, first learning how to shift.

"Okin helped by scouting out the bakery Lindsay lives above. He just came back to report that he found a few teleportation runes, and he could draw them out for you. I will warn you, teleporting for the first time is a bit jarring."

"Okin…" I stared at the tiny dragon. "When you said real dragon, is Okin…?"

"Yes. Okin is not a shifter, like yourselves. He is a dragon who shares my soul. You could say we are bonded, but it truly goes deeper than that. Okin is my other half." Doctor Logan spoke, smiling, and then began to unwrap the rest of my bandages.

"Good to know. How long would it take to get to them? How far away are they? Am I okay to shift? To fight?"

"Teleportation is instantaneous. They are on the other side of the country, somewhere in Washington State, if I remember my teleportation runes correctly. If you feel ready, I recommend washing off the healing salve and getting dressed before I send you."

I smiled and nodded. "Thank you. I won't take too long." All four Windsors looked at me, all wanting to know the answer to the same question, but there was no question in my mind of who I needed right now. My boys knew it too. As Doctor Chester walked out, I grabbed Henry's hand. "Let's get washed up. This stuff is starting to feel sticky."

"Yes, ma'am." Henry smiled, and we left the other three in the bedroom. The blonde-haired man started the shower and took off his jeans before assessing me. "My queen." He whispered. "Please, let me wash you." He gracefully grabbed my hand and lifted it up to his lips, kissing the back of my fingers.

"Yes, you may." This was exactly why I chose Henry. I needed to feel in control of something, to be doted on as if I were a goddess, and Henry was the one who took the most pleasure in having me be the one in charge. We went into the shower, and I reveled in the warmth of the water against my shoulders.

"You're beautiful." Henry breathed out and grabbed the soap, starting at my shoulders as he stood behind me. "You had us worried." He whispered next to my ear, his hands moving down my arms. "We thought we'd lost you again. Drake was about to start fighting Nick downstairs." The thoughts of how worried my boys were for me created a lump in my throat. I didn't want them thinking I was that easy to lose.

"She'll have to try harder than a couple of spells to take me out." We both knew I was out of the fight once I hit the tree, though. I was dragged back to my worst memories. "I promise to be safer next time."

"Do you really believe we should go after her again so soon? Just the five of us? What if she's not alone?"

Turning around, I looked him in his beautiful blue eyes. "If it looks like we won't win, we'll leave." His arms wrapped around me, and his lips pressed against my forehead. I could feel the sigh escape him, his warm breath against my temples. "We'll treat it as a secret mission." It made him chuckle.

"A stealth mission, Sweetheart."

"Not my strong suit, but I'll do my best."

"I'm afraid your definition of stealth is to leave no witnesses." He pulled away to start washing my hair. A purr escaped me at the feeling of his fingers massaging my scalp. I knew we needed to hurry to catch the coven off guard, but this felt borderline orgasmic. After putting in conditoner, he clipped my hair up and went to work washing the rest of my body. His whisperings of sweet nothings as he kissed my clean skin warmed my heart. Telling me I'm gorgeous, how I make him feel stronger just by being next to him, how I belong to him. The cold tiles felt nice against my back, contrasting with the warm water as I leaned back. Henry stood up, nodding at his handiwork, assuring me I wouldn't feel sticky after the shower. This intimacy is what I missed the most when I was away. Sex was great, but the feeling of belonging to my boys was euphoric.

"All clean, my queen." Once again, he brought the back of my hand to his lips, his long, wet hair cascading down as he did so.

"I love you." Going to my tippy toes, I kissed him softly. His hands went to the back of my head and licked my bottom lip, asking to deepen the kiss, which I gladly accepted.

"I love you, too," Henry spoke against my lips before giving me a quick kiss and turning off the water. Inwardly, I groaned, being reminded we didn't have the time right now.

After we left the bathroom, the other three of my boys waited for us on my bed. "Looking good, Lia." Lany smiled, hopping off the bed. "Ready?"

I stood there giggling, a towel around me and nothing else. "I need to get dressed. I don't think they want to see all of me when I kill her."

"It's a great intimidation tactic." Drake nodded. "I say we should all go naked. No one wants to fight someone they think is crazy."

Looking back at Henry, he'd already dried off, using his own body heat to evaporate the water. "I'll get you something to wear." He kissed the top of my head, and Asher stood.

"I've already picked her out something." Tossing a pair of jeans and a hoodie my way. Once dressed, the tiny dragon,

Okin, waddled in. I still couldn't wrap my head around this dragon not being a child, a mere wyrmling. More questions came to mind as I stared at it. How did it come to exist? Did it hatch? Was it born, similar to how shifters were? What did it mean to be Doctor Logan's other half? Did they share the same brain?

"Do you talk?" I asked it, hoping it could understand me. With a shake of its head, I mentally signed. At least it understood me. It did, however, move its head in a way to signal for us to follow it. Her? Him? I could have sworn Logan told us. Was it a male because Logan was male? Seeing as none of us took a step forward, it chuffed and paced between us and the door. "Okay, we're coming." Asher held my hand as we walked forward.

I could hear Uncle Nick and Aunt Carol talking to Mable in the kitchen, discussing what to do next as we snuck to the backyard. Doctor Logan had raked an area of debris away and stood with a stick in his hand. Okin excitedly flew to him and grabbed the stick, starting to draw on the ground. "Okin will draw the teleportation runes, but I recommend not stepping on it until he's finished. One wrong line and you can end up on the complete opposite side of the earth."

"That's a hazard." Lany shook his head.

"Nondruidic magic tends to have…" The doctor tapped his chin, looking down at Okin before deciding on his next words. "Additional rules. Any slight change could have a slightly different effect. But, not to worry. I'll have Okin go with you in case something happens, and he needs to draw it again. Also, be sure to hold hands when you step through; otherwise, only one of you will be teleported, and we will have to redraw the circle again." Said circle of runes started to glow blue, glowing brighter the closer to finishing the circle the little one got. "Okin will also be able to talk to me once you all get there. My assumption is they went to reconvene and think of a new plan. You all need to go in quietly; look for their plans. If you are able to take a mage out in the process, I won't blame you. When you've done what you need to, Okin and I will bring you back."

Looking at my boys, I saw the same look on each of their faces. It was how both vague and specific the doctor was being. It gave us a cover story, a reason other than killing a mage to go. As they looked at me, we all nodded, agreeing on the plan.

"Sounds like a plan." Drake put a hand on my shoulder while Asher held my hand. Warmth spread across my chest as my love for all of them showed. Drake, the alpha, who was always there to push me to my best. Henry, the one who always brought the snacks and made sure I was hydrated. Landon, the one who could always make me laugh, despite the bad influence he could be, Finally, there was Asher, the man who was always right by my side to make sure I never felt alone, even if it was something he didn't really want to do. I kissed each of them, relaying how much I appreciated each of them for being here with me. "We've got this." Drake leaned down, whispering in my ear. Okin flew to my shoulder after finishing the circle.

"Be safe." Logan smiled, and we grabbed hands, taking a step into the blue circle.

Instantaneous it was, but fuck if my stomach didn't feel it. I could only compare it to the feeling of an elevator, both starting and stopping, moving while spinning. The five of us bent over, hands on knees, as we do our best not to see our lunch again. "That was… Something." Lany groaned.

"Where are we?" Slowly looking around, I admired the mansion in front of us. And here I thought the Windsor's place was fancy. The driveway we stood in curved into a full circle, with the building curving halfway. In the middle of the circular driveway was a fountain. The water fell from a spiraling sun onto what looked like wooden logs, and the water cascaded off, disappearing under the pebbles surrounding the fountain. Behind us, the road curved directly onto the main road.

"How do you suppose we're getting in?" Lany asked.

A small chirp at my shoulder caused me to look at Okin. The tiny dragon jumped off my shoulder and flew towards the end of the house, curving around the back. "Do you think it wants us to follow?" Asher's question hung in the air as we all stood there, gaining our composure.

"I don't…" My voice trailed off as I saw the dragon fly towards us from the other side of the house.

"Logan says it knows a way in." Drake looked up from his phone and nodded at Okin. "Lead the way, little fella." It flew back to where it came, causing the rest of us to run after, doing our best not to be seen. Though we didn't know where any cameras were, or if anyone was watching them. "Logan says there is a service entrance on this side that's unlocked."

Of course, they had servants. The glass door with a few steps leading up to it was open, and the smell of food wafted out. "Is there anyone in there?" Okin flew right in, seemingly, without a care in the world if we get caught. Crouched, we all slowly walked along the wall with Drake at the front. Henry silently pointed out things that might make noise or things to watch out for. The Alpha crept up the stairs and almost fell backwards as something came flying at his face.

"Okin!" Asher growled. "This is no time for games." It tilted its head, as if not understanding.

"It's clear." Drake dusted off his pants, sending a glare to Okin.

"Maybe, if one of us shifts, we could talk to him?" I thought out loud. I knew it wouldn't make sense for any of us to shift since we were all the size of an SUV when fully shifted. I just wish we could talk to it.

"That's a great idea." Henry nodded. "However, we should do that at a later point in time."

"Yeah, I thought about that after I said it." Once inside, we looked around. Not only was it a kitchen, but it was as if we'd just walked into the back of a restaurant. There were clear cooking, prep, and clean-up areas with a door at each end of the large room.

"This way. Logan says Okin didn't spot anyone in the servants' area, so we should be okay to move around." The boys nodded, and I watched as they moved as if they'd done this before. When the fuck did they become secret agents? After Drake turned a corner and gestured for us to follow, I realized they've done this before, in their virtual reality games. We all entered what seemed to be the foyer with a spiraling staircase. "Up there." Drake pointed, and before he could move forward, I shifted, my back growing wings, allowing me to fly up to the top. This wasn't one of their games, and I wasn't going to allow them to think it was. What we were doing had serious consequences for staying too long. We needed to get the jump on them. There was a small hallway with a small door to the right and a larger, double door to the left, a little further down the hall.

Slowly twisting the handle of the smaller door, I opened, praying it wouldn't make noise. Inside was a broom closet, almost empty of supplies. My boys were at the top of the stairs when I looked back, following my lead of using our wings to not make noise. We didn't need to catch a creaky step and alert anyone we were here. "Leave…" A loud, male voice spoke, making my heart leap into my throat. "Except, you two." With the sound of the door further down the hall opening, I ushered my men into the closet.

I didn't get the door all the way closed before I heard voices coming closer. "Who the Hells was that?" The voice sounded familiar, though I couldn't place it.

"George has only spoken about him. He's the one who grants us the use of magic. Or, at least that's who I think it was." This time, it was a female voice speaking. Taking a peek through the door's opening, I saw the man who creeped me out at the farmer's market when I first arrived back. No wonder he creeped me out.

"That's Lindsay's dad," Drake whispered in my ear. Him? My eyes bulged out as I looked back at him. All four of my men's eyes had shifted so they could see clearly in the dark. I paused as I mentally noted who was in here.

"Where's Okin?" Shit. Shit. Shit. What if she were found out while we were hiding here? Sure, this house was big, but we also didn't know how many people were in this house. Seeing Lindsay's dad, the woman he was talking to, and a younger man walk down the stairs, and not hearing anyone else, I slowly opened the door, making sure the coast was clear before moving towards the door they just left from. It was then that I saw Okin at the end of the hall, pretending to be a statue on a side table. Something told me it wasn't the best way to hide. I don't think these people take too kindly to dragons, let alone would use them to decorate their household. I thanked the Lord that Okin wasn't spotted.

"While you're waiting, make sure you try to remember everything you know about both the Swallows and the Windsors." The powerful male voice spoke again. He was definitely on the other side of this door. A shiver of fear went up my spine for the first time since we arrived as I touched the door's handle. "Look, George," The one-sided conversation continued. "If you don't have those damned dragons out of my hair soon…" There was silence for a few moments that begged me to open the door and take a peek. Closing my eyes and taking a calming breath, I clenched my fists. Now was not the time to get caught. The power radiating from that room sent another shiver up my spine and put my ears on end. A loud thud echoed, followed by the sound of several books falling, making me jump. "Next time, I won't be so nice. I already have too much to deal with right now." The threat lingered through the air, and I was dying to know who was behind such power.

Looking back at the closet door, I saw Drake watching me. As we locked eyes, he shook his head. I knew he could hear the conversation as clearly as I could, and we both knew the one-sided conversation was coming to a close. He didn't want me taking any chances, but this could be the only chance I got. He didn't understand how much power I felt from the other side of this door. Pressure on my hand caused it to turn, and I watched as Okin turned the nob. It was silent as the door slowly revealed a tall man with pitch-black, feathered angel wings on his back. Their movements told me they weren't fake. I was in the presence of a fallen angel. Fuck me. My stomach churned as I caught a glimpse of his shimmering golden eyes and the scars across his face that traveled down the right side of his neck. I watched as he traced the wall's intricate designs with his finger. When he completed tracing the sigils, the wall disappeared, almost as if a key opened a door. The angel took one last look at the man on the ground and sneered. "Humans and their incompetence." He scoffed before walking through the portal, and the wall appeared again.

When, who I assumed to be George, groaned, and the sound of books being knocked around echoed in my ear, I sprinted back to the closet Drake was still watching me from, no doubt giving a play-by-play to his brothers. I fell against him as heavy footsteps exited the previous room. "Amber!" The pain was evident in his voice. "Where's the healing tonic?" I looked back at the closet door where Henry silently eased it closed, slowly enough that it wouldn't be noticed. A green light emanated from under the door, and the knob twisted.

"I have some down here, Hon!" The woman from earlier yelled. The knob stopped turning, and his heavy footsteps faded as he descended the stairs. "Okay. The coast is clear." I whispered and opened the door. Tiptoeing into George's office, I paused at seeing the bookcases and scattered books on the floor.

"What happened in here?" Asher whispered.

"A fallen angel." I guessed, remembering the entity in awe. The boys looked around the office as quickly and quietly as they could while I examined the sigil on the wall that the angel touched.

"A what?" Drake turned around quickly.

"There was an angel with black wings in here." From the corner of my eye, I saw Okin freeze and heard the buzz from Drake's phone.

"Logan wants you to describe the angel."

My hand went across the sigil, wondering how this magic worked. It couldn't be too hard if the tiny dragon could do it with a stick. "He didn't have a halo." My words began to trail off, but gestured with both of my hands at my back. "Huge, black, feathered wings."

"He caused this?" Henry was looking through the books on the ground as he asked. Landon stood in front of him, looking through the books still on the shelves that weren't knocked down.

"Yeah. If anything, he's the thing we're after. He seems to be the one making decisions."

"Great." Asher rolled his eyes. "We have to go after a fallen Angel whom we don't even know how to get to."

"Maybe Logan knows a thing or two?" Henry chimed. "He was saying something about Angels this morning." Henry nodded at Drake. "Ask 'em."

"Or..." I started to trace the sigil's lines and, to my surprise, it lit up as I finished one of the sigils. The light blue shimmering spread as my finger glided through the indents in the stone. The four men dropped what they were doing, forgetting about being stealthy as they watched me closely.

"Is that what I think it is?" Lany asked. None of us noticed as a man around our age with slicked back, black hair walked around the corner into the office while reading a thick book. "Hey, Dad, when it specifies dragons, does that include the shifters as well?" He looked up to see us turn around in shock. This was it. We were caught. I put my hands up, as a child would when they were caught taking a cookie from the cookie jar. Behind me, a low hum emanated. Taking a moment to glance behind me, I saw the wall wasn't there, though I didn't remember finishing tracing the circle.

Praying a small thanks, I grabbed the back of Henry and Lany's shirts and, in turn, they grabbed Drake's and Asher's arms. Taking a step back, I felt my stomach lurch, twisting and turning as we teleported somewhere else. "Fuck me." I groaned, falling to my knees. I didn't know where we found ourselves, and frankly, I didn't care at this moment. All of my focus was on not vomiting. New Rule. Teleportation is once a day max.

"Not right now, baby." Drake held his head, taking the teleportation better this time.

"Next time, can we get a little bit more of a warning?" Henry sighed, leaning back against the cold wall.

"Whose office is this?" Asher took a step forward to look around the room. A simple dark wooden desk was in the middle of the room, and the walls to the left and right were full of books. Was this the fallen Angel's office?

The one door in the room opened, revealing a woman with long, black hair holding a stack of file folders full of papers. Her void black wings relaxed as she sighed, relief showing on her face. It was only when she looked up and saw us that she tensed up again. "Who are you, and why are you in my office?" She and I looked each other up and down. Could I take on a fucking fallen angel? Thankfully, I wouldn't be doing it alone, being reassured when I felt my boys take a step closer to me.

The power emanating from her felt too similar to the earlier angel. The urge to answer her overpowered the impulse to attack. "I… am…" Drake's alpha presence helped my mind focus, calming me. "Amelia Ann Swallow. I am here." I looked around, still not knowing where here was. Was this the afterlife? Is that where the angels were? On the other side of the veil? "We," I gestured to my boys, "are here by accident. It was only now that I recalled Logan's warning about making a transportation rune wrong. It wasn't my fault; I didn't know that not finishing one had the same effect.

"Where exactly is here?" Asher glanced around the room. The black wood complemented the reds and browns on the walls.

The woman set the folder on the desk and nodded in understanding. "Typical humans." She shook her head.

Not allowing the woman to finish her words, I glared, anger rising. "Dragon." I would not be underestimated by this fallen angel. The fear of standing in this being's presence suddenly gone. Drake probably had a hand in overcoming the fear. I wondered if he felt her effects at all.

The woman blinked several times in shock. "Dragon?" She looked around as if trying to find a small dragon similar to the one Logan had. "Where?"

"*I* am a dragon," Amelia clarified. My mind went to Okin. The last I had seen of him was sifting through the papers on the desk in George's office. Did we accidentally leave him behind?

"Dragon shifter," Henry added, remembering all of Logan's talks.

"Dragon shifter? Is that an actual thing?" The woman asked before clearing her throat. "Well, then you should know a thing or two about what I'm about to say, so I don't have to explain it *all* to you." She smiled. "I am Vanessa Void Black, head of the Dark Angel High Council, and you have somehow traveled into the Angel Dimension."

Next Upcoming Book

Butterflies

For an

Angel

Featuring:

Vanessa Void Black
Five Dimensions Timeline: November 13th, 2006

About The Author

Born and raised in Arizona, the blue-haired woman known as Saraphinia loves to spend what time she can going on adventures and trying new things. Some of her pastimes, other than writing, include motorcycle riding, sticker collecting, and playing Dungeons & Dragons.

She can be found yearly at Phoenix Fan Fusion in various self-made cosplays. Given enough time and money, Saraphinia wishes to travel and go on many more adventures to see the world.